DARK
DESTINY

*The Sleeping Beauty story
your Mother never told you*

DARK

DESTINY

*The Sleeping Beauty story
your Mother never told you*

A Novel by
Kym Hackenberger & Melody Lowe

Wicked Witch Productions, LLC
wickedwitches.tripod.com

Prologue

Centuries ago, in a time when brave princes battled forces of evil to rescue beautiful princesses,

When fairies and wizards roamed freely, weaving spells and bestowing magical gifts,

When the king was the unquestioned law of the land, and all obeyed his proclamations,

When marriage was arranged by families of noble blood to strengthen kingdoms and uphold tradition,

Into this time was born to good King Byron and Queen Isabelle, a beautiful princess, Ealasaid.

Royal subjects gathered from near and far to celebrate the joyous occasion.

But soon, the little princess, a helpless babe in her cradle, fell victim to an evil spell cast by the Queen of Darkness.

Now the castle sleeps, a mercy bestowed by the good fairies of the kingdom, that those who slumber may not know the pain of the spell come to rest on their beloved sleeping beauty.

All fear the Queen of Darkness and the strength of her magic.

They do not know the story of Dark Queen Elspeth...

An innocent heart spurned, a life cruelly taken, a love forever lost...

A woman with nothing to hold but her vengeance.

Chapter 1
The Magician

Five-year-old Elspeth bounded through the tall grasses and flowers of the field, her long white hair rippling in the light breeze. Far behind, her heavyset Nurse sputtered and wheezed with every step. The Nurse turned a wistful eye back toward Elspeth's home, Castle Rookskrieg, atop a nearby hill.

"Ohhhh…why did I let the child talk me into this?" she rasped. Turning her eye back to the field, the old woman panicked. Her royal charge was far ahead. "PRINCESS ELSPETH, YOU STOP THIS MINUTE!"

Oblivious to all but the allure of the forest, Elspeth was soon out of the Nurse's sight. She paused at the edge of the trees to pick up a solitary rose that appeared at her feet. The rose was purple. Carefully pinching the stem between her little fingers, she brought the flower to her face and inhaled. She closed her eyes, allowing the scent to carry her to a place of magic – a place without Kings and Queens and Nurses and castles. A place where she was free to roam the hills and forests, to whirl until she was too dizzy to stand, to drink in the full light of the sun without walls to block the rays.

When she opened her eyes, a pair of shiny dark boots stood where the rose had been. She leaped back, dropping the rose. The boots belonged to a tall stranger. A purple hooded cloak covered his otherwise-black garb.

"Hello, Elspeth." The stranger pushed back the hood on his cloak. His fair hair and pale skin stood out against the darkness of his clothes. Elspeth was transfixed as he knelt to retrieve the fallen rose.

"Please don't be afraid," the stranger continued. "My name is Jethart." He sank to one knee, eye-to-eye with Elspeth. The little princess reached for the rose in his hand.

"Do you want this?" he asked. With care, he placed it in her hand, guiding her fingers around the thorns. She looked into his eyes and smiled.

"Would you like another?"

Elspeth nodded. Jethart put his hands together. Closing his eyes, he raised them to eye-level, palms up. A second purple rose appeared in his outstretched hands. Elspeth drew back as he offered her the flower. He smiled.

"You have nothing to fear, dear Princess. Did you know that you're very special?"

Elspeth shook her head.

"We are very much alike, you and I. You have a gift inside of you. And someday, if you like, I will teach you to use it."

Jethart smiled as he cupped Elspeth's cheek. Their eyes locked for a long moment.

"ELSPETH? PRINCESS ELSPETH! WHERE ARE YOU?" The Nurse's shrieks broke the spell.

Jethart rose as he handed Elspeth the second flower. "Remember me, Elspeth. We shall see each other again."

Clutching the roses, Elspeth watched as he swirled his cape and spun into the air, disappearing in a purple whirlwind. The Nurse, struggling to stay on her own feet in the wake of the wind, caught the little girl.

"Who was that evil magician? Did he talk to you?" The Nurse grabbed the roses. "And what's this? You know you are not to talk to strangers, let alone accept gifts from them!"

Hurling the roses to the ground, the old woman grabbed Elspeth's hand and dragged her in the direction of the castle, scolding with every step. Elspeth looked back at the roses, their remaining petals fluttering in the breeze. She wondered when she would see the stranger again.

Chapter 2
A Royal Wedding

Fifteen years later, the stone floors of Rookskrieg Castle shook with merriment as zealous gypsies tumbled and danced among the wedding crowd.

From the shadows of a corner, twenty-year-old Elspeth cast a sullen gaze across the room. "It should be my day," she thought bitterly, as her eyes came to rest on her sister. The gypsies had encircled the bride and groom, dancing and singing, as the clapping of the crowd bolstered the celebration.

The sound of her father's commanding voice pulled her from her miserable reverie.

"A toast!" He bellowed. "A toast to my beautiful daughter Isabelle, and her husband, Prince Byron. May they live a long life and bring forth many sons!"

The wedding crowd responded with cheers. Elspeth side-stepped the splash of mead as cups clashed in toast, withdrawing further into the recesses of the great hall. She stung from her father's remark. She knew it wasn't intentional but it hurt nonetheless. Isabelle was always referred to as the beautiful one, and their younger sister, Lillith, the clever one. Elspeth was nothing special, simply the eldest. The plain, pale, sulking girl who didn't quite fit in to the royal role decreed by her order of birth.

"There you are!"

Elspeth cringed at the accusing tone in her mother's voice. She knew she was in for a lecture.

"Elspeth! Why do you hide in this corner? This is a celebration. You should be dancing!"

"I do not care to dance, Mother," she sighed. "I have no reason to celebrate." Elspeth knew it probably wasn't the best response, especially given the look in the queen's eye, but her underlying anger wouldn't allow her to bite her tongue this time. "Is not your sister's wedding reason enough?"

"It should be my wedding day. I am the eldest. It is not fair that Isabelle wed first. She should have been made to wait!"

The queen heaved a great sigh, than taking a deep breath, tried to maintain an even tone with her rebellious daughter. "Would you deny Isabelle and Prince Byron their happiness because Prince Malcolm has not agreed to a date for your wedding?"

Elspeth sulked in response. She knew it was useless to argue. She'd had this discussion with her mother a thousand times, and the Queen never seemed to understand her side of it.

"Prince Malcolm cannot be forced to choose a wedding date," her mother reminded her. "And why should he? Look at yourself. Dull hair. Dull colors. You make no effort to make yourself more attractive."

Elspeth looked down at her dress. She thought it complimented her long, silvery braids. The gray satin was simple in cut and fit her well. But a look at her mother's eyes told her otherwise. What was it she'd said when Elspeth picked out the fabric?… "A nun's robes"…

"What does it matter, Mother? He pays me no attention… not like Byron pays to Isabelle. Malcolm would rather play cards and dice with his friends than dance with me, yet I am the one chastised for being aloof. It isn't fair!" she cried.

"No, Elspeth. You are the one who is unfair. You pity yourself because Malcolm pays you no attention. You want him to be like Byron. But look…"

The Queen drew Elspeth's attention to the wedding couple. Elspeth felt her heart sink as she watched the loving moment shared between Isabelle and Byron. It was obvious that Byron worshipped her sister. It was a feeling that Elspeth longed for, but knew she would never have with Malcolm. Her father had chosen him simply as a matter of treaty between Rookskrieg and Talonsbay, not because Prince Malcolm loved her. Her thoughts were interrupted by her mother.

"Look at how Isabelle is attentive to Byron. You must give of your heart in order to receive, Daughter."

The Queen prayed her words would reach Elspeth, but all Elspeth could think of was her own shame at being raffled off to the highest political bidder.

"You don't understand, Mother! Why should I be forced to marry a prince who cares only for my dowry and nothing for me? Why can I not join Lillith in Elfhame and learn magic and healing arts with her and the good fairies?"

Elspeth knew her words would fall on deaf ears, but she yearned desperately to go to Elfhame. Lillith had been in residence there for the last five years, learning the ways of the Fae. Elspeth could think of nothing more exciting for a young woman to do. She felt drawn to that magical world, as if she had a distant memory of life there. And it was certainly a life far more appealing than being an obedient wife to Prince-not-so-charming.

The Queen rolled her eyes. "The magic again? We have been over and over this, Elspeth. You know it is your royal duty to represent your father's kingdom with honor and humility. Your father's holdings go with you to Malcolm. Poor Isabelle takes nothing to Byron except the love in her heart. And Lillith? Learning magic has always been your youngest sister's destiny. It is her lot in life to serve others."

She paused a moment, waiting for Elspeth to absorb her words. "I pray that you would learn to love Prince Malcolm, or at least honor him out of respect for your father."

"But, Mother..."

"ENOUGH!" Her patience had been sorely tested, and the Queen would tolerate no more discussion. "This is not a point to be argued. It is your responsibility... your royal destiny."

"Very well, Mother." Elspeth knew speaking further would only make things worse. "As you wish. I shall seek out Malcolm and do my best to win his attentions."

The Queen smiled in triumph as she watched Elspeth leave the safety of the dark corner and venture out among the guests.

While her mother could insist that she spend her time at Malcolm's side, she couldn't make her partake of the celebration activities. Elspeth slunk through the crowd, keeping a low profile. She had no desire to be drawn into the ring of dancing gypsies, and cringed when she heard her name shouted. She reluctantly raised her head.

"ELSPETH! ELSPETH!"

A young bubbling redhead waved her dainty arms. Elspeth raised her hand and waved in response. It was Lillith! They embraced as they came together.

"Oh, how I've missed you!" cried Elspeth. "You really have no idea."

"And I you, Sister."

Retiring to a nearby empty settee, Lillith chattered incessantly, as was her habit. Elspeth laughed at her. She missed the magpie warbling of Lillith in the castle. It was too quiet without her.

"I love this dress. This satin is wonderful."

"You should tell Mother that," Elspeth replied. "She referred to it as 'Nun's robes'."

"Oh, not at all! Why it's…"

"Lillith. Never mind about my dress. Tell me about Elfhame! Is it wonderful?"

"Oh, yes. It is. But, I still have so much to learn."

"You know you are destined to be the most powerful healer in the realm. How I wish I could join you!"

"I know. I wish that you could, too, but we each have our destiny, Elspeth."

"Yes," Elspeth sighed, "as our Mother is so fond of reminding me." Elspeth fell into a contemplative silence.

"Elspeth?"

"Yes, our destiny," Elspeth continued. "And speaking of destiny, I'm afraid I must take my leave for now and find Prince Malcolm." Elspeth stood, taking a moment to brush a few stray hairs back into place and shake the wrinkles from her skirt, anything to prolong her meeting with Lillith. But her sister saw through her ruse. Rising, she gave Elspeth a quick hug and sent her on her way.

"Of course you must be off. Godspeed, my Sister."

With an encouraging wink, Lillith sent her off to find her prince.

Chapter 3
Prince Not-So-Charming

Elspeth didn't have to waste time looking for Prince Malcolm. Wherever the men gathered to play cards and dice, that's where he was to be found.

She hesitated at the door of the room, watching him. She knew there were other princesses in neighboring realms that were jealous of her seeming good fortune. Malcolm was quite handsome. There was no denying that. His face was tanned and chiseled, and his muscles bulged from his years of training with the soldiers of his father's army. His long black hair fell in waves that begged for girls to run their fingers through it.

He could have had his pick of princesses, but being a dutiful son, he let his father decide. Now, it seemed to be a choice that displeased him, and he took out his discontent on Elspeth at every opportunity.

Sliding quietly along the wall, Elspeth crept up to stand silently behind Malcolm's chair. The men ignored her as they tossed about gold coins and cards, calling out their bets.

At last the game ended, and Malcolm angrily threw his cards into the center of the table. Elspeth thought she had joined him without notice, but she was wrong. He immediately turned to her.

"What do you do here? You curse me with bad luck!"

"I'm sorry, Prince Malcolm, but surely it is just the luck of the cards."

Her words were no solace to him. He'd lost a large pot of coins. "What do you want?" he snarled. Elspeth hesitated. She didn't want to be here.

"Speak up or leave!"

She seriously thought of leaving, but knew she'd only incur the wrath of her Mother if she did. Feigning bravado she didn't at all feel, Elspeth began. "I... I thought perhaps we could share a dance... in honor of Isabelle's wedding."

With another snarl, Malcolm picked up the cards and began to deal them. "Can't you see I am busy? I have no care for dancing."

"Then maybe a walk in the rose garden?"

Malcolm ignored her request as he finished dealing the cards. Encouraged by a wink from one of the players at the table, Elspeth tried again. "Perhaps we..."

Malcolm blew up, slamming his fist on the table. "Just because we are betrothed, Elspeth, you cannot expect me to cater to your every whim."

Startled by his response, Elspeth stepped back. Her emotions were like a taut string of thread that was very close to breaking... first the wedding, then the lecture from her mother, and now this. Taking a deep breath, she tried to respond in a manner that her mother would find appropriate. "But... I would like to share some time with you this evening."

Sneering, Malcolm spoke loudly to his friends. "Then go warm a bed, Elspeth, and wait for me there. I'll give you time when I am ready."

Elspeth's face turned deep red. "How could he!" she thought.

His friends hooted with laughter, knowing full well other women were already waiting for Malcolm's attention tonight. Having shamed Elspeth publicly, Malcolm smiled with delight as he returned to the card game.

Tears welled up in Elspeth's eyes. She had to get out of there. She ran toward the door, praying that a black hole would swallow her up and take her from Rookskrieg forever.

Blinded by her tears, she could barely make out the shape in the doorway. Twisting to avoid running into the person, she cried out in alarm when a strong hand grasped her arm, stopping her departure. The hand gently turned her around, and took her straight back to Malcolm's side.

She wiped away the tears, and looked at the stranger. There wasn't much to see, his face hidden by the hood of the long purple cloak he wore. Elspeth attempted to pull her arm free and leave, but the stranger held her gently in place, patiently waiting for Malcolm's attention. Malcolm steadfastly ignored the pair.

At last, the stranger spoke. "I find your remarks extremely rude, Sir. I believe you owe this lady an apology."

Elspeth was stunned. No one had ever defended her before, especially against Malcolm. She looked from the stranger to her betrothed. Malcolm continued to ignore the man.

"I EXPECT that you will apologize to this lady... now," the stranger repeated. It was not a request. It was a demand, made with quiet authority.

Malcolm was not used to this tone from anyone. He looked up at the stranger with defiance. "It's no business of yours. Leave us."

The stranger leaned forward. His eyes glared out from the dark recesses of his hood, unsettling Malcolm.

"I am making it my business. You WILL apologize."

The demand had turned into a challenge. The stranger stood back up to his full height and held Malcolm's stare as the Prince rose from the table. Elspeth was fearful. She'd seen Malcolm on the tournament field, and in duels. She knew he was a formidable force to be reckoned with. She did not know this stranger, and now feared for him.

She pulled at his arm. "I beg you, Sir, leave this matter be. It is of little consequence."

She felt the stranger shift as she looked to see Malcolm's reaction. When she looked back, her gaze was caught in the stranger's eyes. He had pulled back his hood, revealing hair and skin as pale as her own. She felt a stirring.

"You are wrong," the stranger said in a gentle tone. "You are the star for which all evenings wait, dear Princess, and I will not tolerate your radiance being diminished by one not worthy of you."

Elspeth's heart leaped. Never had anyone spoken such words to her. She smiled.

"HOW DARE YOU!" Malcolm boomed, seeing her reaction. "Who do you think you are to speak to MY betrothed in such a manner?"

The stranger turned to Malcolm, responding with feigned innocence. "You mean as opposed to the way YOU speak to her?"

Malcolm's face reddened and his eyes bulged. Elspeth thought he would go into an apoplectic fit as he sputtered, searching for words.

"You… you… arrogant bastard! I should have your tongue cut out. Who are you anyway? Who invited you to this celebration?"

The stranger responded in an aloof manner. "Does it matter so much to you?"

"Whoever you are, you have no respect for authority. I believe I shall have to teach you a lesson."

Malcolm's friends at the card table quickly scattered, pulling the table with them. With the floor cleared, Malcolm drew his sword, pointing it at the stranger's heart.

The stranger stood calm and motionless. Elspeth could not believe his bravery as he faced Malcolm's sword, especially since he held no weapon of his own.

"I suggest you consider your action, Sir, for whatever you give will find countless ways back to you."

Malcolm refused the stranger's odd invitation for withdrawal. He never backed down from a fight. Smiling, he responded, "Then perhaps I shall have the pleasure of watching you suffer a thousand times!"

With no further warning, Malcolm thrust the sword at the stranger, who dodged it with catlike agility.

Stepping behind Elspeth, the stranger pushed her toward the door. "Leave, Princess. This place is not safe for you." Elspeth ran to the doorway, but she couldn't bring herself to leave. This strange man had defended her.

Holding tightly onto the doorjamb, Elspeth watched as the stranger continued to dodge Malcolm's sword. She hated the men who were cheering Malcolm on. Couldn't they see that he was wrong? He should have apologized, at least to the stranger.

Elspeth watched in fascination as the game went on: Malcolm thrusting, the stranger dodging, the men cheering. Soon the stranger tired of the game, and he stopped. Elspeth held her breath, expecting Malcolm's sword to find its mark. She cried out when the stranger grabbed the blade in his hands.

Malcolm was more surprised than anyone. He watched as blood dripped from his opponent's hands gripped tightly around the blade. The stranger didn't seem to notice.

"It would be much less work to apologize," the stranger chastised.

Anger fueled Malcolm's response. "I have NOTHING to apologize for! Release my sword so I can run you through with it!"

"Certainly," the stranger calmly replied. He loosened his grip on the sword, but Malcolm could not move it. It was held in place by a purple aura that began to swirl around the stranger's hand, making its way up and down the length of the blade. The men were silent, staring in awe at the spectacle.

Elspeth was spellbound. The purple tendrils seemed to call to her. She took a step forward, then suddenly recoiled in horror. The stranger had released the blade. Malcolm found himself holding a large writhing snake. With a cry of disgust, Malcolm threw the snake to the ground. He looked back at the stranger.

The stranger raised his palms to Malcolm. There were no cuts, no blood. Malcolm stared in disbelief. All watched in amazement as the stranger swirled his cloak tightly about him and disappeared in a purple whirlwind, rising into the ceiling.

With the stranger gone, Malcolm looked back to the floor. The snake was gone, and his sword remained in its place. Malcolm picked it up, tentatively studying the metal before sheathing it.

Elspeth stared at the ceiling, watching the purple mist dissipate. She was not expecting Malcolm's attack.

"YOU! This is all your fault!" Malcolm was standing in front of her, and grabbed her roughly by the arms, shaking her. "You planned this, didn't you?"

Elspeth feared for her life. She had seen Malcolm's anger and knew his strength. "I… I don't know what you mean…" she cried.

"Because I refuse to dance with you, you seek to make me a fool!"

"No!… I would never…" she whimpered, futilely attempting to protect herself.

Malcolm tossed her away. She landed hard against the stone wall. She cowered there, fighting the tears that threatened to return.

"You spoiled, ugly wench! I don't know why I tolerate your presence! Your father should have sent YOU away to Elfhame. At least Lillith is pleasing to the eye."

Unable to control her emotions anymore, Elspeth gave in to her tears. Sobbing, she sank to the floor.

"I tire of your childish tears," shouted Malcolm. Grabbing her up, he shoved her toward the door. "Get out of my sight!" Turning away from her, Malcolm returned to the card table. With a look of malice, he dared anyone to challenge his actions.

Chapter 4
Magic in the Moonlight

Elspeth ran to the rose garden as fast as her feet would carry her. From the time she was a young child, this was her favorite place. She would revel in the sweet fragrance of the blooms in spring as it wafted through her bedchamber window above. Now, she found herself on a stone bench, too distraught to notice the beauty of her surroundings. The muffled sound of laughter and music floated from inside the castle, taunting her. She did not notice the owl watching from a tree branch above.

Suddenly, a shadow fell over her, and she looked up to see the handsome stranger who had come to her rescue a short time before. As she swiped the tears from her face, he extended his hand to her.

"Would you do me the honor of dancing with me, Fair Princess?"

Taking his hand, her eyes never left his face as she rose and stepped into his arms. Quietly, they began to dance to the music filtering from the celebration. When the dance ended, the stranger offered his arm and led her down a path through the rose garden. After a short distance, they came to a stop. They turned to face each other, silhouetted against the moon, full blossoms surrounding them.

"May I see you again?" the stranger asked.

"I…I cannot." Elspeth turned away, unable to meet his gaze. "I am betrothed, and it wouldn't be proper."

"Please… meet me again. Here, in the rose garden."

"But… my parents… Malcolm…"

The stranger placed his finger under her chin, turning her face toward his. "I shall be forever heartbroken if you refuse to see me."

She looked at him deeply, drinking in the elixir of his eyes.

"I could not bear to be the cause of a broken heart."

"Until tomorrow night, my love."

She returned his smile. Slowly, he backed away and faded into the darkness.

Chapter 5
A Secret Love

Elspeth paced the floor of her bedchamber, listening to the activity in the hallways.

"I wish you would all go to sleep!" she harshly whispered at the door. Vexed with waiting she threw herself on the bed. A moment later, she sat upright, surprised. The castle was suddenly quiet, as if her wish had been granted.

She hurried to the window, flinging open the shutters. Anxiously, she searched the rose garden below. It had been a week since she had last seen Jethart. A long, horrible week filled with her mother's tirades about the injustices suffered by Prince Malcolm at the wedding. As if Elspeth cared! She'd hardly even thought of Malcolm since that night. All of her thoughts had been focused on the time when Jethart had said he would return.

Below in the rose garden, Jethart had waited patiently in the shadows, knowing she would come soon. He had watched the castle intently as each window darkened, until at last, the inhabitants of the castle slept. All but one. He stepped into the pale moonlight so she might see him clearly.

Elspeth's heart raced as he came into view. Happily, she waved, and he waved in response. She quickly closed the shutters and headed into the dark corridors.

Jethart met her at the garden gate, near the forest's edge. He drank in the sight of her running in the shimmering light. She was radiant - breathless and blushing, as she hurried to his side. Jethart took her hand, kissing the back of it, then turned it over to gently kiss her palm.

Elspeth sighed. The gesture, so small, spoke volumes to her heart.

"Come with me, Princess."

Elspeth hardly heard what he said. Jethart's voice seemed a part of the night, like the flutter of dark wings, or the croak of the frogs. His dark velvet tone was like the harmony of an alluring song.

"What?" she whispered.

"Come with me, into the forest."

Elspeth hesitated. "Are you sure it's safe?"

"Of course," he whispered.

He led her through the dark trees, to a clearing ringed by toadstools.

"Where are we?" she whispered.

"At the dance."

Elspeth gave him a questioning look. Surely he was jesting. They were in the middle of the forest, alone.

"But…"

"Just dance, Elspeth," he interrupted. Jethart pulled her into his arms, twirling her around the toadstool ring, then into the center of the clearing. He hummed a whimsical tune in her ear, and she quickly fell into the rhythm of his dance. Within seconds, hundreds of fireflies surrounded them, twinkling like the stars in the sky.

Elspeth sighed again, enjoying the romance of the moment. She settled her head in the curve of Jethart's neck, comfortable in his embrace. Closing her eyes, she dreamed of magic.

When Elspeth woke the next morning she was not sure if the dance had been real or a dream. Rolling over, she saw a purple rose lying on her bed stand. She smiled to herself, knowing the dance had been real. She quickly arose and hummed the whimsical dance tune as she dressed for the day ahead.

The day seemed to last forever, and try as she might, Elspeth could not keep her thoughts from straying to her next planned rendezvous. She anxiously watched for the setting of the sun. It couldn't come soon enough to suit her.

When at last dusk came, Elspeth hurried to the rose garden. She sat on a stone bench, hugging her knees to her chest as she watched the garden gate.

A large white owl was perched on the stone fence, watching Elspeth as she patiently waited. Its eyes never wavered from her as the last rays of sunlight gave way to the rising of the moon. After a while, Elspeth noticed it.

"What do you do there, Sir Owl?" she asked lazily. "Do you spy on me?"

"Woooooo?" answered the owl.

Elspeth giggled. "Why you, of course, Sir Owl."

The owl spread his wings and took flight, making a circle over Elspeth's head. She reverently watched the bird's graceful ascent followed by a dive into the nearby forest.

When she turned her attention back to the garden, Jethart stood at the gate.

"You look like a wood nymph resting there."

Elspeth blushed as he joined her on the bench. She was not used to his compliments, and most particularly since she had never heard such compliments as he gave bestowed upon anyone. Every word he uttered seemed magical.

"Are there wood nymphs where you live?" she asked. Elspeth had realized earlier in the day that she didn't know anything at all about Jethart, except his name. She needed to know more.

"A few," he shrugged. "Outcasts from the forests of Elfhame."

"Outcasts?"

Jethart shrugged again in response. "I guess."

It was obvious he didn't want to discuss wood nymphs. "Where is it that you live?" Elspeth asked, hoping for more information.

"A nearby realm."

"Which one?"

"The one that awaits the honor of your presence, dear Princess." He took her hand, kissing it. The kiss seemed to cloud her mind. She thought no more of questions, only of his lips. He continued to shower kisses on her hand, then her arm, making his way to her shoulder. Just when she thought she would melt into a puddle, he stopped.

"Come," he said. It was a command.

Taking Elspeth's hand he led her into the forest. Elspeth giggled with excitement. Maybe he was taking her dancing again. She soon realized they were moving in a different direction. At last, they stopped at a pond in the forest. Elspeth gasped at the sight. At the edge was a gondola for two, pulled by a flock of black swans.

"Careful," Jethart cautioned, as he guided her into the boat. Elspeth settled in, as Jethart climbed in beside her. As the swans began to pull the small gondola, Jethart busily wove a spell. Elspeth watched in delight as purple tendrils of mist rose from his fingers and took the shape of a bouquet.

"For you, my love," he announced as he laid the flowers in her lap.

Elspeth was speechless. After a moment, she realized her lack of manners. "Oh… Th… Thank you, Jethart," she stammered. Jethart raised a finger to her lips.

"Hush, my love. Don't speak." He put his arm around her shoulders and pulled her close. Again, Elspeth's head found the curve of his neck, and again, she closed her eyes and dreamed of their many magical meetings.

Chapter 6
Happiness Interrupted

Elspeth sighed wearily at her window. It was the wee hours of the morning, and she couldn't sleep. The never-ending rain had prevented her meeting with Jethart for several days. Frustration was setting in and she feared she would never see him again. As she watched the rain pouring from the dark sky, her eyes fell on the circles of flight made by a large white owl. The same white owl who kept her company in the garden every evening until night fell and Jethart arrived.

Elspeth's eyes grew suddenly large as she realized the owl was headed straight for her window. She stepped back in horror as the bird smashed into the glass. She heaved a sigh of relief when the pane held. But her relief was only temporary, for seconds later the owl dove toward the window again.

Elspeth watched again in horror as the latch broke open and the large bird crashed into her room. She screamed as she fell to the floor to avoid being bombarded by the creature. Forcing herself to peek through her fingers covering her face, Elspeth gasped. Before her, a purple mist slowly took the shape of Jethart.

"You?" she gasped. "You are the owl?"

"Yes." Jethart took her hand and pulled her into his embrace. "And I could not bear to spend one more night away from you," he whispered into her ear.

"Nor I," she breathed. "I have missed you terribly. You can't imagine."

"Yes, Elspeth, I can," he answered.

Elspeth looked into his eyes. She was greeted by a passion she had never seen before. He pulled her closer into his embrace. "I love you, Elspeth. I have always loved you."

For the first time, Jethart kissed her lips. A long, passionate kiss, such as she had never known. Her body tingled. Jethart ended the kiss, and pulled away. "I must go."

"I… I don't want you to," Elspeth whispered. It was all she could manage. She could barely breathe.

"Don't worry, my love. We shall be together soon," promised Jethart. He pulled his cloak around him, and dissolved into a purple mist, quickly taking the shape of the white owl. Elspeth watched as he made a circle around her then headed out the window. As he passed through the shattered frame, shards of glass floated up from the floor, each one settling into its respective place until the window was magically repaired.

Elspeth rushed to the sill and threw the casement open. "I love you!" she called out after him. She ignored the pelting of the rain as she watched him fade into the darkness.

Closing her window, Elspeth fell into her bed. "How could it be," she wondered, "that the night passes so quickly, yet the day seems to drag on forever? Especially the days of Malcolm's visits!" Her hours spent with Jethart were never enough. Thoughts of flowers, fireflies, and tender kisses filled her head as she drifted off to sleep.

Elspeth awoke with a start as she realized it was late afternoon. Her countless nights of secret rendezvous' were catching up with her. She hurried to dress for the evening meal.

A short time later, Elspeth sat quietly at her mother's side as they awaited the arrival of the King. The Queen studied her daughter's face, noting an underlying aura of content – something she had not noticed before.

"You seem quite happy recently, my dear."

Elspeth was startled from her thoughts. She had been immersed in plans for her next meeting with Jethart. "Oh… yes, Ma'am… I am," she stammered nervously, as if she had been caught in the act of meeting her love.

The Queen nodded. "Things are better with Prince Malcolm, then?"

Elspeth's face darkened. Her mother could not be further from the mark. She hadn't even thought of Malcolm in the past weeks, except for the days she was forced to spend time with him during one of his numerous visits to Rookskrieg. Malcolm's father had recently died, and there were many political points to be settled with his ascension to the throne of Talonsbay. Malcolm looked to her father for guidance.

"Well?" her mother questioned.

"I suppose," she answered, feeling guilty for lying to her mother.

"Of course things are better with Prince Malcolm!" Her father's authoritative voice filled the room as he entered, overhearing their conversation. The servants scrambled at his arrival to quickly bring the meal.

As their plates were filled, the King continued.

"I spoke with Malcolm just this afternoon. With the passing of his father, he naturally inherits the throne. Now that he is to be crowned King, he is duty-bound to take a Queen. Therefore, he has set the wedding date."

Elspeth struggled to hide her horror as her mother squealed with delight. She had become so immersed in her secret tryst that she had completely forgotten her betrothal. It no longer seemed real to her. A life with Jethart was what she wanted and the only thing she could imagine.

"Oh, how wonderful! Isn't that wonderful news, Elspeth?"

"Um... yes. Yes, Mother," she lied.

"Yes! Oh, I am so excited! We must start planning at once."

"At once, indeed," her father interjected. "The wedding is to be in one month."

Elspeth was heartsick. How could she have let this happen? She should have told Malcolm she didn't want to marry him. But no, he wouldn't have listened to her. She could never stand up to him like that.

"Elspeth?" The King questioned his daughter. "Elspeth, are you well? You look faint."

Indeed, she did feel faint. It felt as if her heart had stopped beating altogether. "I'm fine," she answered weakly.

"I'm sure it's just the excitement of the news," offered the Queen. "Why don't you lie down for a bit, dear?"

"Yes, perhaps I will," answered Elspeth. She stood, taking a moment to brace her shaking knees before continuing to the hallway.

She managed to contain her tears until she was well out of sight and earshot of her parents. Stealing away to the back servants' stairway, Elspeth ran out to the rose garden. Her tears continued to fall as she nervously paced the garden paths, waiting for Jethart to arrive. She formulated a hundred plans to run away as she waited, and discarded them all. She could never leave. She was trapped by a treaty of marriage, and could not dishonor her father. Her heart broke into a thousand pieces as she faced the truth. She must give up Jethart and follow her destiny.

Chapter 7
A Date is Set

Darkness had set in and still Jethart had not arrived. Elspeth started down another path, searching, eager for the feel of his arms around her. He emerged from the shadows behind her. She jumped when he placed his hand on her shoulder, then recovered her composure.

"I'm glad you are finally here!" She threw her arms around him, holding him tightly. "I've received the most dreadful news," she began.

"What news, my Princess?"

"MALCOLM! He has finally set a date. What am I to do?"

Jethart stepped back, loosening her hold on him. He looked into her eyes.

"Do you love him?"

"Of course not! How could I love a man who treats me as he does?"

"Only a monster would treat such a beautiful princess so." Jethart reached for her hand and drew her close. "Marry me, Elspeth. Be my Queen."

Overcome, Elspeth struggled to reply. "How... how can I? My parents have planned this marriage to Malcolm for years!"

"Let them continue to make their plans, my love. We shall make our own."

She looked at him questioningly.

"Trust me, Elspeth."

Letting her go, he rubbed his hands together with a flourish. They were quickly surrounded by a swirling purple aura. As he pulled them apart, a white dove appeared. Elspeth could see that it carried a silver ring with an amethyst stone in its beak. The bird hovered momentarily on the mist between them, then dropped the ring in her hand. She watched as it flew, disappearing behind the garden wall. Lovingly, Jethart took her hand and slid the ring on her finger.

Chapter 8
The Moment of Truth

Radiant in her white silk, Elspeth's father escorted her down the cathedral aisle. The royal guests stood and watched as they walked, her long train trailing behind her. Elspeth forced herself to breathe. When they reached the altar, her father kissed her hand, then gave it to Prince Malcolm. Together, the couple turned to face the priest, and the ceremony began.

"Dearly beloved, today we celebrate the union of two realms through the joining of Prince Malcolm of Talonsbay and Princess Elspeth of Rookskrieg. We pray that this union will bring great prosperity and peace to all corners of the combined realms."

The priest turned to speak directly to Malcolm.

"Prince Malcolm of Talonsbay, do you take this Princess to be your wife and future Queen, bound in royal service to you and the subjects of your realms?"

"I do."

"And Princess Elspeth of Rookskrieg, do you take Prince Malcolm as your bound husband and future King, promising to obey him in all manners of service to the royal house and subjects of his realms?"

Elspeth stood quietly for a moment, her face strong and serene.

"No. I will never be bound to this man."

As the guests gasped and murmured among themselves, Malcolm's face darkened and contorted with anger. He opened his mouth to speak, but was interrupted by a turbulent purple whirlwind swirling down the aisle, making its way toward the couple. Thunder and lightning struck around it, shaking the floor and walls. The shrieks of the guests were barely audible over the noise of the whirlwind.

Elspeth jerked her hand free of Malcolm's. She turned and calmly faced the force as it stopped between them. All watched, stunned, as the whirlwind dissolved into the shape of Jethart. He took Elspeth's hand and drew her to his side, placing an arm around her waist.

Malcolm finally found his voice.

"YOU! Be gone from here, you foul demon!"

Jethart faced Malcolm, and stared directly into his eyes.

"Demon? Everyone here is not as they appear, Prince Malcolm. You treat this woman shamefully. You dare to ridicule a princess worthy of your own rank, yet you call ME a demon?"

Malcolm struggled for words, but found himself speechless.

"Then again, perhaps you are correct," Jethart continued. "It takes a master of evil to recognize the evil soul you hide behind your crown of nobility. I will not allow you to destroy Princess Elspeth with that evil."

He turned to address the guests.

"I take the Princess with me. She will be MY Queen and rule at MY side in a realm where she will be honored and respected by all. No more will she be subject to the apathy and snobbery of your petty nobility."

Facing Elspeth, he continued.

"Come, my love. Your new realm awaits you."

With a sweeping bow, he placed a kiss on the back of her hand. He then pulled her close, wrapping his long purple cape about her, and the two began to spin, slowly at first, then faster and faster, dissolving into a turbulent purple whirlwind. As the whirlwind vanished through the ceiling, a flash of thunder and lightning put the entire crowd back on their heels.

After the couple disappeared, Malcolm's face bespoke the murder he was contemplating.

Chapter 9
The Dark Realm

Elspeth was surprised at how quickly their transformation had occurred. One moment she was enveloped in Jethart's embrace at the church altar, and the next, she was here. But where was "here"?

Stepping back from Jethart's arms, Elspeth turned slowly, taking in her surroundings. They were in a great hall, far larger than the hall at Rookskrieg, or so it seemed. It was difficult to gauge. The hall seemed empty compared to the busy castle of her father.

The high walls were covered with tapestries. Marble benches were placed at intervals at the floor's edge, and plush cushions were scattered about. Elspeth turned toward the north wall. Worn steps led up to a raised dais. There, in the center, was the largest throne she had ever seen. Carved in black marble, and adorned with silver gargoyles and dragons, it obviously belonged to a rich and powerful king. She turned back to Jethart.

"Where are we? What is this place?"

Jethart took her hand. "This is my home, Elspeth. Our home now."

Elspeth cast her eye about the room again. A feeling of uneasiness came over her as she noted several small, dark figures hidden in the shadows of the tapestries. Jethart followed her gaze, and smiled to himself. He knew who waited there. With a nod of his head, he beckoned the creatures from the shadows.

Several imps and goblins scurried to hide behind the safety of his cloak.

Elspeth struggled to maintain her composure. She wondered what these hideous creatures could be doing in Jethart's home, and even more, why they should run to him for protection.

She attempted to quell the quiver in her voice and carry on a normal conversation. "I've… never seen a castle quite like this," she stammered.

"It is different from most, though I'm sure you've heard of it," Jethart replied with a confidence that assured her he was Master here.

Elspeth took another cautious glance about the room.

"It is known as Dubh Rathgart," Jethart continued. "The Black Fortress."

Elspeth laughed with relief. She should have known this was an illusion. "The only Black Fortress I ever heard of belonged to the Dark King, and he is but a legend."

Jethart bowed before her. "At your service, my lady."

Elspeth continued to laugh, but only for a moment. She suddenly realized this was no illusion, and Jethart was not pretending. She looked again at the dark creatures peeking at her from behind him and took a quick step backwards.

"No!… It's not true, Jethart," she gasped. "It can't be. The Dark King is a horrible monster. A demon!"

Jethart took a step forward, attempting to take her hand. She pulled it away, stepping further from his reach. He stopped. He didn't want to upset her. He knew he needed to make her understand without rejecting him. He had loved her far too long to lose her in this moment.

"Do I look like a monster, Elspeth? Have I been horrible?"

Elspeth searched his face. "No... Of course not," she replied.

Jethart slowly crossed the distance between them, taking both her hands in his. "I am the Dark King, but I am no monster. And this realm is not the dark place others would have you believe. It is a refuge for those who are cast out and shunned by other worlds." He nodded toward the group of goblins and imps in the center of the room. "You asked me once if wood nymphs lived where I came from. They do - naughty nymphs, angry fairies, witches, goblins, trolls... all those not wanted in other realms. Our subjects are not evil, Elspeth, just mistreated and misunderstood. In this realm they live in peace under our protection. They are free to be happy... and a bit mischievous at times."

Now, he waited anxiously for Elspeth's reaction.

Elspeth could tell by the look in his eyes that he spoke from his heart. He cared for these creatures. He understood them, as he understood her. She looked again at the dark and motley group.

One of the goblins met her gaze, and stood up as straight as he could. He adjusted the mismatched armor he wore as he cleared his throat. With as large a sweeping motion as his twisted body could muster, he

37

bowed to Elspeth. "Welcome, Dark Queen," he announced.

As he bent, his helmet went crashing to the stone floor. The sound echoed loudly through the great hall. He was immediately set upon by his comrades. They chattered and screeched as they smacked him, chastising him for ruining their important moment. Elspeth watched the melee with wonder and amusement. How could she have feared these tiny creatures? They seemed more like a group of small children fighting in a nursery over some favored toy than demons. Stepping past Jethart, she rescued the goblin from his friends, taking his small hand in hers.

"Thank you, Sir," she said. "I'm certain I shall be quite happy here."

No words could have made her new subjects happier. Now, they surrounded her, each one vying for her attention.

"My name is Irwing," announced the rescued goblin. "Please, Dark Queen, let us show you the castle!"

"That would be most wonderful," answered Elspeth. She laughed as they hurried to see who could grasp her hands first. She glanced back over her shoulder to see Jethart smiling at her. She returned his smile as she followed the chattering chorus of creatures from the great hall.

Jethart breathed a sigh of relief as she left the room. His fears were at rest. He knew now she would stay with him forever. He turned to leave the room, and noticed an imp hidden in the shadows.

"Ignatio? Come out of there."

The small imp slid from behind the tapestry, but still clung to it. Jethart went to his side and knelt down to his level.

"Ignatio, are you not happy to meet your new Queen?"

Jethart was surprised at the timid creature's sudden outburst. "We don't need Queen!" he shouted. "We have King Jethart!"

Jethart measured his words carefully. He didn't want to upset Ignatio anymore than he already was. The little imp had been sorely treated before arriving in Jethart's realm and he deserved respect.

"You must understand, Ignatio. Every King should have a Queen, and Elspeth shall grow to be a wise and caring one."

"No care!" the imp shouted. "She change things. Send away!"

"She will bring a woman's touch to our Fortress… a quality it is sadly lacking."

Ignatio stared angrily at Jethart.

Jethart felt the full weight of the imp's stare. He contemplated his next move. "I want you to do something for me, Ignatio."

Ignatio responded as Jethart had hoped, a spark of excitement in his questioning eyes. "What, my King?"

"I want you to plant a rose garden for her."

Ignatio was immediately disgusted. "YUCK! Flowers stink! No like flowers! We don't need." The small imp moaned and groaned and continued to whine with hardly a breath between his angry words. Jethart feared Ignatio's tirade would never end.

"IGNATIO!"

The commanding voice stopped the small creature mid-word. He cowered under Jethart's gaze. "Yes, my King?"

"Elspeth is here to stay," he admonished the imp. "Do as I say and make her welcome. It is my wish."

The imp knew there was no arguing. A king's wish is a king's command. "Yes, my King," he answered meekly, then slunk back into the shadows.

Chapter 10
A Kind of Magic

Elspeth followed warily behind Jethart, picking her way carefully along the crooked stairway. Even after nearly a month at Dubh Rathgart, she was finding hidden passages and dark corridors that hid the secrets of Jethart's realm.

"Watch your step, Love."

Elspeth glanced down at her feet to side-step a wide crack in the worn stone. "Where are you taking me? I don't remember this stairway."

Jethart reached back, taking her hand. "It leads to my study, Elspeth. A place I want to share with you." He paused for a moment, giving her time to join him on his step before proceeding. "There are things you must learn, my love, in order to be a true Queen of the Dark Realm. It is time for you to learn our magic."

Elspeth's heart skipped a beat. She could hardly believe her ears. She had always wanted to learn magic and had been so jealous of Lillith when she left for Elfhame. "You're going to teach me magic?" she breathed, praying she had heard him correctly.

Jethart smiled at her quiet exuberance. "Yes. In order to control the realm."

He pulled her into his arms as they reached the bottom of the stairs, and Elspeth bounced with excitement. "Oh, Jethart!" she exclaimed, as she planted a kiss on his cheek.

"My, my. What an eager student you are," he laughed, as he turned and opened the heavy wooden door that filled the space behind him.

Elspeth held her breath as the door creaked open. The faint glow from inside pushed its way into the hallway, forming a purple halo around Jethart. In that moment, Elspeth could feel his connection to the magic of his realm. A second later he stepped aside and allowed her to enter.

She treaded softly, following a worn path in the ancient carpet, side-stepping the stacks of magical artifacts that struggled against each other for prominence in the room.

"Many secrets are hidden here." Jethart's velvet tone floated across the room and pulled her attention back to him. "Secrets I have wanted to share with you from the first day I saw you." He stepped quickly along the room's path to join her. "I have loved you your whole life, Elspeth."

Elspeth's heart fluttered as Jethart pulled her into his arms and kissed her. Nobody had ever professed to love her as he did, and she knew she would never love any other. She melted into his arms, and almost fell when he suddenly pulled away. "I have a special gift for you, my love."

"Another?" she asked. "Jethart, you spoil me. What is it?"

"Hmmm. Perhaps I do spoil you," he admitted, "but this gift is truly special."

Jethart took another step backwards, and the magical room seemed to grow and give him space as he grabbed the ends of his purple cape and stretched it out. After a moment, he pulled it in, wrapping it around his body like a set of bat's wings. Elspeth could feel the room vibrate as the magic flowed through the atmosphere. Seconds later, Jethart unwrapped the cape and let it fall back to reveal Elspeth's gift. He smiled as she gasped.

Hovering in the air between them was a beautiful silver staff. It was etched with magical runes up and down the length of it, and a crystal orb rested at the top.

"It's beautiful," she murmured.

"Take it, Elspeth." His words were a command. She tentatively reached out, barely touching the shaft. The orb immediately began to hum, emitting a faint lavender glow. Elspeth quickly pulled her hand back, and watched in amazement as the glow faded away. She reached out again, and the orb glowed a bright purple as she closed her hand tightly around the shaft.

"It is your link to the magic of our realm," Jethart said solemnly. "Your source of knowledge and power."

Elspeth shifted her gaze from the glowing orb to Jethart's eyes.

"Take this staff, Elspeth. Become one with the spirit it holds, the spirit of a wise and passionate Queen. Never lose it, as it is your only source of power. Without it, you shall be as mortal as I am without my cape."

Elspeth held the staff in both hands, inspecting each magical rune in turn. "Thank you, Jethart," she whispered.

As she finished her inspection of the gift, she finally looked back into Jethart's face. "Now you must teach me to use it."

As the days went on, and Elspeth reveled in happiness in the Dark Realm, her father sulked in misery at Rookskrieg. He had sent many troops out to search, but there had been no sign of her, or the Dark King. And, once again, Prince Malcolm was at his castle gate, demanding another audience.

With a sigh, he conceded to see the angry man. "Let him in," he told his steward.

A few minutes later he watched Prince Malcolm as he stormed through the door of the throne room, thrusting his cloak at one attendant, and shoving another. The elder King took a deep breath and steeled himself for the inevitable attack. "Prince Malcolm," he nodded, "Welcome."

Malcolm completely disregarded the greeting, and stomped his way to the top of the King's dais. He waved a finger in the old man's face. "For God's sake, it's been a month since she ran off with that devil! Have you no control over your own daughter?"

The King averted his eyes in shame. "I had no idea she was in league with the Dark King. Had I known, I…"

Malcolm slammed his fist down on the armrest of the throne. "You promised her – AND THIS KINGDOM – to me! She must be brought back and your obligations met!"

"I have no way to…"

"FIND A WAY," Malcolm screamed. As quickly as he had stormed into Rookskrieg, he stormed out, leaving a path of fear and despair behind him.

As her father spent his days in anguish at the chaos in his kingdom, Elspeth spent hers in her element. Lillith and Elfhame no longer mattered. She was learning the magic of the Dark Realm under the guidance of her true love. It seemed to flow into her being naturally, and she loved the feeling of power it gave her. As she finished a spell in a small cauldron, a miniature black dragon riding a purple mist appeared above it. She smiled, knowing she had succeeded at her assigned task.

"You are an excellent study, my love… as I knew you would be," encouraged Jethart.

He moved the cauldron aside and opened an ancient text. Elspeth grew pensive as she watched him flick through the pages. Her sudden quietness drew Jethart's attention. He watched her fidget for a few moments from the corner of his eye, waiting for her to speak.

"Jethart?"

"Yes," he replied.

"Are you going to teach me to place a curse?"

Something about her entire mood troubled him. He turned to study her for a moment. "Why would you want to learn such a thing?"

"Oh, it just seems a good thing to know… For protection only, of course," she answered as matter-of-factly as she could.

"Protection, Elspeth," he asked, "or vengeance?"

Elspeth quickly averted her eyes, as his drilled through her. "You wouldn't be seeking to 'protect' yourself from a certain King, would you?"

At the mention of Malcolm, her eyes flashed with hatred and anger. "And what if I am? If anyone deserves to be cursed, it is him! He brings nothing but misery to all around him!"

"As I know he did to you, my love," Jethart acknowledged. He took her shoulders and turned her so she squarely faced him. "I do not teach you magic so that you may use it to harm others," he admonished. He placed his finger under her chin and raised her tear-filled eyes to face him. "Always remember, Elspeth. Once you step upon the path of vengeance, your destiny is sealed. The pain you visit on others shall revisit you a thousand-fold."

She searched his face, and understood why those cast out of other realms sought safety here. Jethart understood them as he understood what she felt for Malcolm. Wrought with emotion, she fell into his arms, sobbing into his chest, knowing that he would keep her safe and make everything alright.

But everything was not alright. Malcolm had already stepped onto the path of vengeance, and he was tired of Elspeth's father trying to peacefully resolve the situation. He had already decided that the Dark King must return what was rightfully his. It mattered not what the old king's most recent letter said, Malcolm was ready to take action.

He crumpled the parchment into a ball and slammed it into the table. His officers seated at the great table worked to suppress their reaction, knowing any statement would enrage their King further.

"That old fool!   I must do everything myself! Gather me an Army… At once!" he screamed at his officers.

"I shall take back what is mine!"

Chapter 11
The Gift of Life

Elspeth grew strong in the magic she was learning from her husband, as they spent countless days together as master and pupil. Her love for him grew in equal measure.

One afternoon, they sat side by side in a window seat as Elspeth read from a worn magic text. Jethart watched over her shoulder as she read, pointing out passages of particular interest. The third time he reached toward the book, she grabbed his hand.

"I beg you, Sir, to stop disrupting my studies!"

Jethart smiled. "It is the teacher's prerogative."

Wrapping his arms around her, he kissed both sides of her neck. She laughed softly and closed the book.

"Jethart?"

"Yes, love?"

"I have a special gift for you today."

Jethart sat up, his curiosity piqued.

"A gift… for me?"

Elspeth nodded.

"What is it?" Jethart was like a child trying to contain his excitement.

"A gift of life, Jethart. I carry your son."

The Dark King's surprise gave way to a jubilant shout as he grabbed and hugged her tightly.

"A son? Are you certain?"

"Yes. The magic within the staff tells me so."

Jethart jumped up and pushed the windows open wide. Hanging his head outside, he shouted to Irwing in the courtyard.

"IRWING!"

"What is it my King? Is there trouble?" Irwing had never known his King to shout from the windows.

"No! Wonderful news! Spread the word... a prince is to be born!"

Irwing began jumping up and down. Letting out a whoop, he ran from the courtyard.

As a mood of happiness engulfed Dubh Rathgart, Talonsbay was overtaken by a sinister fury. Malcolm was at the blacksmith's, wielding a newly-honed sword as the smithy and captain of the guard looked on. He waved it through the air, and flexed the steel testing its strength. Finally, he slammed it down on the anvil, causing it to shatter. The smithy was terrified as Malcolm threw what remained of the sword to the ground.

"AGAIN! Try again! Don't you understand? I need a sword powerful enough to destroy a demon!"

The smithy bowed. Picking up the pieces of the sword from the ground, he threw them into the fire.

Meanwhile, the sun shone warmly in the Dark Realm as days of happy bliss passed. Elspeth tended the rose garden Jethart had made for her with the help of Ignatio. Together they cut the purple blooms, gathering a bouquet. But Ignatio was not paying close enough attention, and reached for the same bloom as Elspeth, cutting her hand with his pruning knife. She screamed, dropping her things and clutching her wounded hand. Ignatio drew back in fear, crouching close to the ground.

"Sorry… Sorry Queen! Not mean to!"

"You idiot! Look what you've done!" she was overcome with anger.

Elspeth did not hear Jethart as he came up from behind. He watched the confrontation.

"Was accident!" Ignatio continued. "Please don't shout!" The small creature held his hands to his ears as he crouched.

"You could have cut my hand off! Ohhhhhh! You are so CARELESS, Ignatio!"

"Sorry! Sorry!"

The Queen stepped toward Ignatio, but stopped when she felt Jethart's hand on her shoulder. She turned to face him.

"There is no reason for anger," he chided. "Here… let me see your hand."

He took her hand and examined it, then looked into her tearful face. "Don't cry, love."

As he kissed her cheek, Ignatio despaired. He knew his King worshiped the Queen, and he feared retribution for the accident. He quickly scurried from the garden.

"It's just a flesh wound," Jethart continued. "Let me take care of it."

Rubbing his hand over the wound, a purple aura appeared around it. When he removed his hand, the wound was completely healed.

"I'm sorry, Jethart." Elspeth fought back more tears. "I didn't mean to shout. I know it was an accident, but it frightened me. I'm sorry, Ignatio…" As she turned to apologize, the little imp was nowhere to be found. "Where did he go?"

Jethart's voice was reassuring. "I'm sure he didn't go far. You can talk with him later. Come, rest for a bit."

Tucking her hand into his arm, Jethart led his Queen through the garden. As they walked, she glanced over her shoulder, searching for Ignatio.

Chapter 12
An Elusive Princess

As Elspeth's days passed happily at the side of her Dark King, a very angry King Malcolm sat on his throne in the Great Hall at Talonsbay Castle. The captain of his guard knelt before him. At Malcolm's nod, the captain rose.

"Have you found her?" Malcolm's tone was demanding.

"I'm sorry, Your Highness," the captain gulped. "We've searched everywhere. No one has seen Princess Elspeth, nor do they know where to find Dubh Rathgart. The Black Fortress remains hidden by the Dark King's evil magic, and the men fear entering the Dark Realm."

Malcolm slammed his fist on the throne's armrest.

"This is unacceptable! Do you hear me? UNACCEPTABLE!"

The Captain struggled to find his voice. "Yes, Sire."

"The Black Fortress must be found!"

"Yes, Sire."

"Redouble your efforts! Every day that passes loosens my grip on Rookskrieg. If she is not found, then my claim to the land must be forfeited. And that cannot happen." Malcolm's voice became menacing. "Do you understand?"

"Yes, Sire. She will be found," the captain promised. After a bow, he turned on his heel and left.

Life at Dubh Rathgart, meanwhile, was idyllic for the expectant King and Queen. But Jethart found himself unable to shake a mounting feeling of dread. He kept his feelings to himself, of course. Elspeth could not be burdened in her present state. One night, as they lay sleeping, Jethart was restless. Awakening, he sat up, and looked over at Elspeth, who slept soundly. He reached toward the bedside table and picked up a crystal ball. As he turned it in his hands, it began to glow, emitting a soft purple light. Mist filled the inside of the globe. As he stared at the mist, it dissolved into a horrific scene of soldiers and goblins engaged in a fierce battle. Jethart rubbed his hands over the crystal, and the image dissipated.

"No," he whispered to himself, "it's just a dream. Nothing more."

He replaced the crystal ball on the table and slid down into the bed, close to Elspeth, laying his hands lightly on her pregnant stomach. He whispered to his unborn child.

"It's just a dream, my son. Nothing shall harm you as long as I am here."

Chapter 13
Lost in the Mist

The next day, the Captain led a small patrol of King Malcolm's soldiers through the thick fog that surrounded the Dark Realm. At each turn, they found themselves at a dead end. The Captain's patience grew short.

"Damn this mist! Is there no sunlight in this hellish place?"

"Let us try back this way, Sir," replied one of the soldiers.

"Is that not the way we came?"

The soldier looked lost. "I… I'm not certain, Sir. I just don't know."

With a sigh, the Captain turned his horse and led the patrol in the suggested direction. After a few yards, they ran into another dark mist. "CURSE THIS PLACE!" the Captain shouted. "Are we doomed to ride in circles forever? BAH! All of this trouble for an ugly princess."

The men continued to search the area about them for an opening. Suddenly, something dropped from a tree above, landing directly in front of the Captain. It was Ignatio. The captain worked to steady his horse as he drew his sword.

Ignatio cowered, covering his head with his hands. "Sir?"

The other soldiers gathered behind the captain, pulling their swords.

"Stay back, demon!" the captain commanded.

"Please sir! You look for Dark Queen?"

The captain hesitated, holding back his sword a bit and motioning to his men to hold fast.

"We search for Princess Elspeth," the captain replied.

"Yes! Yes… HER, the Dark Queen!" Ignatio couldn't hide his excitement or his distaste for the Queen.

"Do you know where she is?" the captain asked.

"She is here."

"Here?" The captain looked around, perplexed.

"In the Dark Realm," the little imp replied. "In Black Fortress at end of path. She is there."

"So we are in the Dark Realm?"

"Yes, my King's land." Ignatio began to jump up and down. The captain threatened the imp with his sword.

"How do we get through here?" he demanded.

"Follow path." Ignatio stretched his little arm before him.

"There is no PATH!" The captain was obviously growing weary of the exchange.

"I show you," Ignatio offered. "I show path and you take Queen."

The captain sat back in his saddle, allowing the words to sink in. Finally he found his tongue. "You WANT us to take your Queen?"

"YES!" Ignatio exclaimed. "Take her! Leave here! Leave us!"

"Somehow, I don't think your Dark King will allow us to take her. He's a powerful sorcerer. He will kill us all."

"You take cape. Then take Queen."

The captain was nonplussed. "Cape? What has a cape to do with taking the Princess?"

"King's magic in cape," Ignatio explained. "No cape – no can hurt you. Take cape and take Queen. Please, sir… promise no hurt anyone… just take Queen."

After thinking it over, the captain withdrew his sword and looked to his second-in-command, who nodded.

"Yes, little imp. We WILL take the cape… and your Queen!"

Ignatio's excitement turned to fear as the captain continued. "And we will also take YOU! You are going to show us the secrets of this cursed place, and help us plan our attack." He grabbed Ignatio and tossed him over his lap in the saddle, clutching him tightly. "Now… lead us out of this Godforsaken place!"

Chapter 14
Love Grows

A visitor would never have believed he was in the fortress of the Dark Realm. The halls of Dubh Rathgart had taken on an air of merriment as the birth of the child drew nearer. Jethart led Elspeth along a sunny passage from their bedchamber to a nearby room. He positioned her carefully among a mob of imps and goblins that laughed and played in her presence. Even the babe growing inside of her seemed to join in the merriment, as her swollen belly bounced in excitement.

"Wait a moment," laughed Jethart as he placed her directly in front of the door, then placed his hands over her eyes. Elspeth held her breath as she impatiently waited. At last, she heard the door swing open, and the chatter of imps and goblins as they spilled into the room. Jethart led her forward a few steps, then dropped his hands from her eyes.

Elspeth gasped. She found herself in a richly decorated nursery. She turned slowly in a small circle, taking it all in. At last her eyes rested on Jethart. He stood proudly next to an ornately carved cradle he had pushed into the center of the room. He gave it a shove and it began to rock in a soothing rhythm.

"Oh, Jethart," she cooed.

"What do you think, love?"

"It's so beautiful." Tears began to fall from her eyes as she stepped into his embrace. She placed a hand on his cheek and tenderly kissed her husband.

"The rest. The rest!" one of the imps screeched, interrupting the romantic moment. The others joined in, dancing in a circle around the couple and the cradle. Their childishness only added to Elspeth's happiness on this day.

"Wait a minute. Quiet down! Quiet down!" Jethart shouted to be heard above their din. "There is more."

"More?" asked Elspeth. Jethart had given her so much already, yet every day seemed to bring a new gift or new blessing. She couldn't imagine any other life but the one she shared with him.

Jethart reached into the cradle and pulled out a package, handing it to her. She carefully untied the ribbon that held it closed. As she let the wrapper fall away, a full-length purple cape spilled across her hands – an exact replica of the cape that Jethart wore each day.

"I don't understand," puzzled Elspeth. "A man's cape for a baby?"

"No. For a prince," answered Jethart as he pulled her close once again, and began to rub her swollen belly. "I place this gift in your special keeping, my love. When the time comes for our son to learn the magic, it will be his link to power. I've taken special care to bind a spell of wisdom and protection to it."

"But why give it to me?" asked Elspeth. "Surely this gift should come directly from you to our son. You will be his teacher."

"I think there is much he will also learn from you," he replied, and placed a kiss on her forehead.

Chapter 15
Paradise Lost

Jethart woke with a start. He immediately looked to his side to see that Elspeth slept quietly. "Just another dream," he whispered to himself. He attempted to roll back over and return to sleep, but sleep eluded him. He tossed and turned as a feeling of trepidation gnawed at his heart.

He sat up on the edge of the bed, careful not to disturb Elspeth. He picked up a crystal ball from the bedside table and rolled it back and forth in his hands for a few moments until the mist inside revealed its secrets. He peered closely as it revealed a great dark shadow, leading a large army. He studied it until he could make out the shadow. It was King Malcolm and his face was maniacal as he led his army up the dark, winding road to Dubh Rathgart. Even the black mist could not dissuade him from his course.

Jethart worried. He knew the malevolent man had been searching for Elspeth ever since he had brought her to the Dark Realm, and he had worked at placing many spells of protection around her and their child. He had hoped they would last until Malcolm gave up, but the crystal ball revealed that Malcolm had no intention of letting Elspeth go. Jethart knew a battle would soon be at hand.

"What do you see, my darling?"

Elspeth's soft voice startled him. "No... no... It's nothing," Jethart stammered as he quickly waved a hand over the crystal ball, erasing its images. He set it back on the nightstand, and slid back into the bed next to her. He rested his head on her breast as he caressed her stomach.

"How is my beautiful wife this morning?"

"Ravenous," she answered with a laugh. "Your son begs me to break fast."

Jethart laughed. "And how is my son?"

"He grows stronger with each passing day, my love."

"Have you chosen a name yet?"

Elspeth thought for a moment. "No. I think I must see him first."

The babe jumped beneath Jethart's hand in response to the loud banging at the door that interrupted them.

"What do you want?" Jethart yelled in disgust.

The door swung open to reveal a frenzied Irwing. He dashed into the room. "My King! An army approaches! Very close. Very close!"

Jethart leapt from the bed, and grabbed his clothes, throwing them on as he ran to the window. "Dress quickly, Elspeth! Hurry!"

She scrambled from the bed as quickly as the weight of the baby would let her. She could hear the urgency in Jethart's voice and knew there was danger.

"Irwing, take Elspeth to the dungeons. Hide her there."

Jethart charged from the room before Elspeth could protest his orders. He hurried to their antechamber to retrieve his purple cape. It was gone. He searched frantically. He knew he had to find it. Out of the corner of his eye, he spied a small imp skulking past the door. He yelled.

"IGNATIO!"

The startled imp jumped about a foot, if it was even possible for his small frame to leap that high.

"Yes, King?" he answered in a small voice.

"Have you seen my cape?"

"No! Not see. Not me, King," he stammered.

Jethart sighed heavily and turned his attention back to the antechamber, desperately searching one more time. "All is lost," he whispered to himself. "How can I protect them? I've nothing. Nothing but a few small tricks of magic up my sleeve." He finally gave up his search, knowing he couldn't waste any more time. He had to do what he could to protect his family.

"May faith carry me…" he prayed as he pulled his great sword from its sheath, and lifted a crystal orb from the shelf.

The King's attention turned safely away, Ignatio scurried on down the hallway and around a corner. He rested for a moment, panting and full of fear. He checked under his own cloak to see the splash of purple hidden underneath that reassured him Jethart's cape was safely out of the King's reach. Knowing it was there did not dispel his fear at all. It was not the approaching army he feared, it was Jethart's wrath. He didn't want to anger his King, but he didn't want Elspeth to be here any longer. He had tried to convince Jethart that she should go home, but he wouldn't listen. Now, Ignatio had been patiently awaiting King Malcolm's approach for several days. He had promised to hide the cape, and the human had promised to take the Queen away. The deal was almost sealed, and life could go back to the way it was before. Ignatio steeled himself in that belief and scurried on down the hall.

Jethart found Elspeth standing at the window when he re-entered their chamber. She was watching the approach of the army. She turned when she heard his steps, and she rushed to meet him. Worry engulfed her whole being.

Jethart pulled her close and kissed her passionately, knowing it might be the last time. Without his cape, he knew he had only a slight chance of victory. But, he couldn't let Elspeth know this. "Stay hidden until I come for you, my love."

She nodded, trying to appear as brave as him.

"I have always loved you," he whispered into her ear.

"I love you, Jethart," she answered.

He laid his forehead against hers and placed a strong hand across her stomach, giving the child one last caress. As he pulled away, he took Elspeth's hand and placed one final kiss in her palm.

Without looking back, he retrieved his sword and crystal orb from Irwing and strode quickly from the room.

"Be careful, Jethart! Please!" she shouted after him, unsure if he even heard.

"Come, my Queen," prompted Irwing. "We must be gone to the dungeons. Quickly!" The little imp knew there was no more time for good-byes. The battle his

King had been dreading was finally at hand. He led Elspeth down the steep stairs to the dungeon, and tucked her inside a small cell. Elspeth was reluctant to enter, but at least it held a chair for her to sit on and the floor was covered in straw. Irwing reassured her, "You will be safe here. Please, my Queen. Stay in this room." With a deep breath she entered, but only because she knew Jethart wished her to hide here for safety. She flinched as Irwing closed the heavy door and locked it behind her. The small room seemed to fill her senses with impending doom, and she had to will herself to breathe. Knowing she couldn't just sit quietly with the whole castle in danger, she pushed the chair up to the wall and stood on it so she could see what was happening out in the courtyard of Dubh Rathgart. She was worried. She knew something was wrong, horribly wrong…

Chapter 16
A Hollow Victory

Imps and goblins fell on Malcolm's soldiers at every turn, as the army burst through the fortress gates. The small warriors seemed to erupt from every corner of the courtyard, but they did not matter to Malcolm. He watched in amusement as his soldiers easily cut down the small creatures with their heavy swords. His eye was on the prize. He was searching for the Dark King. He circled the courtyard three times on his great steed, crushing the ugly creatures unfortunate enough to step in his horse's path.

"Where is he?" he screamed. "I want that bastard!"

As if in answer, a flash of lightening rolled across the sky. Malcolm slid from his horse and looked up to see a crystal orb slicing its way through the atmosphere. It shattered into the ground near his feet, releasing a purple mist. Thunder and lightening erupted again as Jethart emerged from the mist, armed and ready for battle.

All action around Malcolm and Jethart ceased. Soldier and creature alike stopped dead in their tracks awaiting the next move.

"What is it you want from me?" Jethart asked.

"My bride," roared Malcolm, his frustration apparent to all, "And your life."

"I'll give you nothing, except one chance to leave here… Now," invited Jethart. He silently prayed that

Malcolm would do just that, but no such luck was on the Dark King's side this day.

With a demonic laugh, Malcolm swung his sword at Jethart, and the battle began anew. With a revived vigor on both sides, the battle raged on violently. Watching the horror, Ignatio now realized that the human army had no intention of simply taking their Queen. They intended to kill them all. He wailed as friend after friend was cut down by the heavy swords wielded by the great army. At last, he resolved to take action.

"LEAVE!" he shouted to the soldiers as he ran through the battle. "GO. No hurt us. LEAVE!" As Malcolm's soldiers came at him, he threw Jethart's cape around his shoulders, immediately transforming into a large terrifying demon that the soldiers quickly scattered away from.

"King Jethart?" he continued to scream, knowing he had to find his King and return his powerful cape.

Inside the dungeon, Elspeth screamed. She had spotted Ignatio with the purple cape, trying to get it to Jethart. He could not win the battle without it. She knew she must do something to help. She jumped from the chair, and dashed to the door, forgetting it was locked, and no amount of struggling on her part would cause the door to give. She was trapped.

Beating on the door, she screamed for Irwing to free her, but he was nowhere to be found. Everyone was in the courtyard except her. She turned, instinctively reaching for her staff, knowing she could use it to free the lock, but it was not there.

"My staff! Where?" Suddenly she realized that with the imp's hurry to rush her to the safety of the dungeon she had left it behind. Elspeth ran back to the door, screaming to be released. It was all she could do.

In the courtyard, with no magic to assist him, Jethart fell victim to the beating he had been taking from the soldiers who had joined Malcolm. Though he fought fiercely and both men had many wounds to show for the battle, Jethart could withstand no more. He dropped to his knees. Malcolm's sword was immediately at his throat.

"Where is she?" screamed Malcolm.

"She is not yours!" Jethart exclaimed.

Anger drove Malcolm as he forced his sword closer against Jethart's skin, drawing a line of blood from his throat. "Tell me where she is! I'm taking back my Princess."

"The Princess is dead."

"YOU LIE!" Malcolm screamed. Enraged he pulled back his sword and thrust it through Jethart's heart with a vengeance. He quickly withdrew it and threw the Dark King to the blood-soaked ground.

"Find her," he roared to his soldiers. "She is here!"

Malcolm turned his back on Jethart, but the dying King's last words, stopped him in his tracks. "The Princess is dead," uttered Jethart, "Long live the Queen…"

Chapter 17
A New Reality

Elspeth screamed as the ax hit the cell door again and again. How foolish she had been to beg for release from the dungeon. Her request had been granted – by the wrong person. Jethart had sent her there for protection, but her screams had brought the soldiers right to her hiding place. How she wished she had remained silent.

She fought and kicked and screamed, but her pregnant body was no match for armed soldiers. They tossed her to the floor, showing no mercy, and drug her out of the dungeon and into the battle-scarred courtyard. She sobbed as she scanned the carnage. Her dear imps and goblins littered the ground, but Jethart was nowhere to be found. She prayed for his safety, even though she knew in her heart it was futile. It was obvious which way the battle had gone. Malcolm's soldiers tied her behind a horse and led her out of the gates of Dubh Rathgart.

Chapter 18
Talonsbay

The next day, Elspeth sat in a chair by a window in a small, dark room. Tears rolled silently down her face as she pondered the fate of her husband. She sat up straight at the sound of the door opening, but refused to turn to see who entered.

"Did you really think I would allow you to just run away?" Malcolm's voice was menacing. Unwavering, Elspeth countered with a question of her own.

"Where is he?"

"Who? … Oh, you mean the demon that kidnapped you? You need no longer fear, my dear. I have sent him back to hell where he belongs." Malcolm chuckled, pleased with the pain his words caused her.

"NO!" Elspeth rose, moving quickly to face her captor. She pummeled him with her small fists. But he grabbed her wrists and wrestled her into submission. Only after she stopped resisting did Malcolm notice she was pregnant. No one had told him... Repulsed, he pushed her away.

"Dear God, look at you! How could you do this to me? I can't marry you now. I would be a laughing stock!"

"You already are!" Elspeth hissed. She ducked as Malcolm swung at her.

"You are nothing! Get out of here! Go back to your father! Let him share in your disgrace!" He grabbed her arm and dragged her from the room.

A few minutes later, Malcolm tossed Elspeth out the castle gate. As she fell to the ground, a crowd began to gather round her.

"You are banished from Talonsbay! Never shall you return! Be gone you demon's whore!" The King's words rang through the stiff air like a death knell. Ignoring the onlookers, Elspeth picked herself up and proudly raised her head. She looked Malcolm squarely in the eye.

"YOU are the only demon I have ever known!" She turned her back on him and, with regal bearing, started walking down the road toward Dubh Rathgart.

A short time later, inside Talonsbay Castle, Malcolm signed a letter, sealed it with wax, and handed it to a messenger who waited at his side.

Chapter 19
The Road Home

Making her way along the rocky, winding road, Elspeth grew weary. Recent days had taken their toll, and she had lost everything. Suddenly she realized she was being followed. She stopped at a sound in the bushes beside the road. Ignatio peeked out, and emerged slowly from his hiding place. His clothes were torn, and his face looked haggard.

"I'm sorry, my Queen."

Elspeth looked down upon the small imp, whose eyes were full of sorrow. She was happy to see he lived. She extended her hand to him. Hesitantly, he took it and they continued on their way up the road.

Along the way, Elspeth continued to gather other stray goblins and imps around her as she walked. The rocky road proved difficult for her tired, pregnant body, and Ignatio caught the Queen whenever she stumbled, preventing her from falling. But the difficult path only served to strengthen her resolve.

As the entourage neared the black fortress, Elspeth encountered several goblins carrying Jethart's body, wrapped in his purple cape, toward Dubh Rathgart. As she followed them, she made no attempt to hide her tears.

Chapter 20
A Dark Day

Meanwhile, at Talonsbay Castle, Malcolm was seated on his throne. A very young, innocent-looking princess named Mary trembled as she was presented to him by her parents. The King nodded his approval. It no longer mattered who he took as his wife. His claim to the lands of Rookskrieg was lost. Elspeth had interfered with his destiny.

The next day, Malcolm married the bewildered young princess in a private ceremony. Following the quick ceremony, King Malcolm and his new bride waved to the crowd gathered in the courtyard, and Malcolm drank in the cheers and adulation of his subjects, who were heard saying:

"He is a hero!"
"Single-handedly killed the Dark King…"
"Destroyed Dubh Rathgart…"
"He will be a great King!"
"A beautiful bride…"
"Prettier than the other one…"
"A great warrior!"

The adoration from his subjects eased the insult of his confrontation with Elspeth. He took pride in the fact that he had destroyed the Dark King and her happiness.

In the days that followed, Elspeth and the inhabitants of Dubh Rathgart constructed an elaborate black coffin with a glass lid. When it was finished, several of the goblins, working together, lifted the coffin bearing Jethart's body into the large chamber of a burial crypt. Amid the crying and wailing from the imps and goblins that filled the room, Elspeth remained dry-eyed. Her grief had passed, and resolve had taken its place. As the coffin was slid into place, she spoke.

"Hush, my children. Dry your eyes and gather your strength. I soon bring a new King into this world. As we wait for him to take his proper place, we shall deal with those who have wronged us by taking away our beloved King Jethart." She paused. Her eyes narrowed. Her voice became sinister. "Vengeance shall be ours."

Chapter 21
A New Covenant

Large clouds rolled through the sky as storms threatened the realm of Rookskrieg. King Byron tried to maintain his calm as the still, humid air closed in around him. He was weary of this constant attack by his advisors. Every meeting brought the same argument lately.

Hidden behind a large tapestry, the Queen's handmaiden, Adeline, also suffered the heat, but she maintained her silence. As the men ended their meeting, she slipped away quietly into a passage behind the curtain, hurrying up the many stairs to Queen Isabelle. She paused for a moment to catch her breath before entering the Queen's chamber.

Adeline entered and offered a curtsy to the Queen, but no words. Her eyes told Isabelle everything she needed to know. The meeting had not gone well. With a wave of her hand, she dismissed her other ladies-in-waiting.

"I'm sorry, Your Majesty. I fear it is bad news. His advisors continue to implore King Byron to put you aside... To take a new queen." She paused for a moment, then whispered. "Some even speak of having you put to death."

Adeline's heart fell at the look of hopelessness on her Queen's face. She felt sorrow for the burden that had been placed on her princess when Elspeth had run away six years ago. Isabelle never wanted to be Queen of Rookskrieg. She and Byron had planned a quiet life in a small realm, not the responsibilities that a kingdom like Rookskrieg required, responsibilities thrust upon them when her father had died.

"They would put me to death for want of a child…" sighed Isabelle. She walked to the window and watched the advisors as they gathered in the courtyard below. "I've tried everything I know to give Byron a child. Herbs. Potions. Prayers. Even asking Lillith to enlist the magic of the fairies. All to no avail."

She turned her attention back to her faithful Adeline. "Do I have any time left?"

Adeline nodded, "Yes. King Byron argued greatly in your defense. He loves you dearly and has no desire to set you aside, let alone have you put to death. But he could only convince the Council to give you until the Winter Solstice to be conceived of a child."

Isabelle turned back to the window. This time she took note of the leaves changing color on the trees, the autumn sunset in the distance. She could feel time slipping away.

"So now they move me to desperation. I had hoped to avoid such a dark undertaking," she said sadly. "Have our horses readied. We will set out at dawn. And Adeline," she admonished, "be discreet."

"I understand, Your Majesty, but how shall we ever find her?"

"I have heard rumors of where the Black Fortress lies hidden in the mists. We will have to rely on the words of others to find our way, Adeline. It's a dangerous undertaking.   We may be lost in the black mists forever. But, the Council has left me no choice. At this point, death awaits me either way."

Chapter 22
An Ominous Reunion

Two cloaked figures on horseback moved slowly along the winding road. Small indistinguishable figures watched them trudge through the black mist from the safety of the ancient trees and hedgerows, but the riders did not notice them. They kept their eyes on the turrets of Dubh Rathgart peeking out of the tops of the rain-filled clouds in the distance.

The image of the riders faded as Elspeth waved her hand over the crystal ball on the table. She was pleased.

"Ignatio!" she called.

Moments later, the little creature scurried into the magical study with a deep bow. "Yes, my Queen?"

"Ignatio, we shall soon have visitors. Make sure my sister finds her way to me."

"Yes, my Queen," he replied. "I will do."

A short time later, Isabelle's gloved hands pushed away the moisture of the inhospitable mist that clung to everything in the Dark Fortress. Then with an immense shove, she pushed open the heavy doors to the Great Hall. Her eyes swept the hall, and she forced herself to remain calm as she caught glimpses of the ugly creatures that scurried to hide behind chairs and tapestries. At last her gaze fell upon her sister. She was not the girl Isabelle remembered from their youth. Gone was the quiet beauty of the innocent princess. In its place, Isabelle saw a proud and angry woman, a woman who still mourned, a woman scorned. She noted Elspeth's black and purple robes, signifying her place as ruler of the Dark Realm. With a deep breath, she approached her sister.

"Isabelle, my dear sister," mocked Elspeth. "I've been expecting you for some time."

"I'm sure you have," she answered, "but let's not bother with pleasantries. Just tell me your price, Elspeth."

"You know the price. Are you ready to pay it?"

Chapter 23
A Bleak Prophecy

Isabelle let her mind wander back to that day four years earlier, when a line of mourners trailed out the door of the mausoleum belonging to Elspeth's and Isabelle's family.

The body of their father, the King of Rookskrieg, lay shrouded on a slab before them. When the other mourners were gone, the daughters stood on either side of the slab, facing each other. Both were attired in the traditional black mourning garb. Light from a torch in a stand by the burial slab illuminated their faces through their thin black veils. Isabelle wept as she leaned over their father. Elspeth regarded her sister stiffly. Isabelle stopped crying and looked up.

"Why do you look upon me thus?" she demanded.

"How?" Elspeth's voice was sarcastic.

"You know how. Please stop."

"Poor little Isabelle." Elspeth nodded toward their father's body. "Now that he's gone, I suppose the lands of Rookskrieg fall to you and Prince Byron."

Isabelle watched intently as her sister began to pace.

"You know," Elspeth continued, "that by rights, the land belongs to ME."

"A right you forfeited when you refused to marry King Malcolm," Isabelle shot back.

Elspeth's eyes flashed. "I would sooner be impaled and left as feed for vultures than join with Malcolm! He shall NEVER get his greedy hands on my land! … It is of little matter," she continued, her voice calmer. "The land shall be mine soon enough."

"You speak nonsense!" Isabelle cried.

"DO I? Tell me, Sister… How many princes and princesses do you and Byron hope to bring into the world?"

"What has that to do with the lands of our family?"

"Oh… everything," Elspeth answered matter-of-factly. "You see, I happen to know that you will conceive – but only after you have surrendered all hope."

Isabelle squirmed as Elspeth got in her face.

"And only with my help," the Dark Queen continued.

Isabelle turned away. "You lie!"

Elspeth walked around so that she once again faced her sister, her demeanor superior. "No, I speak the truth. One year shall pass… then another… then another… until finally, under threat of banishment or even death for your barren state, you will remember this conversation. And you will know that only I have the power to help you. In your desperation, you shall seek me out."

Isabelle was distraught. "I will not listen to any more of this!" Elspeth grabbed her arm as she attempted to leave.

"You SHALL come to me. And when you do, you will already know the price of my help. I will give you a daughter. In return, you will give me Rookskrieg, and your princess shall be betrothed to my son.

"You are mistaken, Elspeth!" Isabelle shook loose from her sister's grasp. "Go back to your Dark Realm! You are not welcome here."

Elspeth was smug. "We shall see." Raising her staff, the orb began to glow, and she disappeared in a flash of lightning. Isabelle fell to the floor beside her father's body and wept.

Back in the present, Isabelle swallowed hard as she faced Elspeth, exactly as her sister had predicted that dark day.

"Yes, I am willing to pay the price." She cringed as an evil smile spread across her sister's face.

Chapter 24
Ossian

Elspeth slowly trailed after her sister, watching smugly as Isabelle quickly retreated to Rookskrieg. She paused on the fortress steps to congratulate herself on her victory.

The sound of laughter pulled her from her dark revelry. She looked up to see Ossian and Irwing bounding from around the corner. She could not help but smile at her beautiful child, only six years old, but already the spitting image of Jethart. He was riding on Irwing's back and swinging a large stick, and both of them were covered in mud. She bounced down the remaining steps to intercept them.

"What mischief is this?" she smiled.

"Mama! Look at me! I'm the King," Ossian shouted.

"Yes, my dear, you are," she laughed.

"We're going to fight the evil king, aren't we Irwing?"

"Yes, Ossian!" said Irwing to his young charge. "We are brothers-in-arms! We shall defeat all who dare to enter our realm."

Ossian waved his "sword" and cheered.

"And what, pray tell, is all of this mud?" asked Elspeth. "I fear you shall never come clean again, child!"

"It's not mud, Mama!" the boy proudly answered. "It's our magic armor. Irwing made it."

Elspeth gave the goblin a look out of the corner of her eye.

"Sorry, my Queen," he answered sheepishly.

Forgiving him immediately, she took Ossian's mud-covered face in her hands. "Go play, my darling. Soon it will be time to prepare for your future."

"Bye Mama! Giddy-up horse!" With a kick to Irwing's ribs they were off again. Irwing quickly galloped away with the young Prince, but not before a reprimand followed them.

"And Irwing… STAY OUT OF THE MUD!"

Chapter 25
An Untimely Death

Meanwhile, though it was day, dreary skies weighed heavily on Talonsbay Castle. Inside a chamber, King Malcolm stood at the bedside of his wife, Mary. She lay still, her eyes closed, cuts and bruises covering her face. As blood trickled from her mouth, Malcolm raised her hand and held it silently.

Mary's chamber maid, Gwendolyn, scurried into the room with a ceramic pitcher of water. She carried it to the table and poured water into a matching bowl. Picking up a cloth from beside the bowl, she dipped it in water and wrung it out. She walked toward the bed with the wet cloth.

"Sire, my husband has gone to fetch the royal physician for Her Highness. He should be here soon."

"I fear it is too late," Malcolm sighed.

Unable to control her sobs, Gwendolyn turned away. Malcolm lowered his dead wife's hand to her side. Neither he nor Gwendolyn noticed five-year-old Prince Roderick in the doorway.

"Mother?" The child's voice pierced the darkness of the room. Gwendolyn rushed to him and began to whisk him away, but Malcolm stopped her.

"Allow the boy to enter. He must know the truth."

As Gwendolyn released his shoulders, Roderick advanced tentatively toward the bed.

"Mother?" He turned to Malcolm. "Why does Mother not answer?"

"She cannot, my son. Your mother is dead."

"But… she will awaken soon?"

Malcolm placed his hand on the boy's shoulder. "No, your mother will never awaken again."

Roderick's little chin began to quiver as he took his mother's hand. A tear rolled down his cheek. "Mother? Mother? It is time to awaken now. You promised a story. Remember? Mother?"

As the reality of the situation set in, the boy laid his head on the Queen's stomach and sobbed. Malcolm turned and walked to the window. Several more servants appeared at the entrance to the chamber. A manservant approached the King.

"Sire? What has happened?"

"Her Highness has been taken with a fever," Malcolm replied curtly.

"But… Sire, I saw her just last night and she seemed fine."

Malcolm did not attempt to hide his irritation. "She acquired the fever during the night. Now, I want you to issue a proclamation that the Queen has died, and Talonsbay is in mourning."

"Sire, what of the boy?" Gwendolyn inquired meekly.

"With his mother gone, he will be sent to Sir Lawrence for training in the military arts."

"But Sire, he is only five years old…"

"Silence!" Malcolm's shout ripped the air. "My command is issued! Now, away with all of you! … And take the boy!" he added.

Cringing, Gwendolyn walked up behind Roderick and took him gently by the shoulders.

"Come, child," she said quietly.

"No! I will not leave! Mother! MOTHER!"

The boy's wailing echoed through the corridor as he was dragged away. Malcolm walked to the window and stroked his chin as he stared out at the dark clouds.

Chapter 26
A Fateful Gift

The halls of Rookskrieg bustled with activity. Ladies-in-waiting, court advisors, and servants rushed back and forth past King Byron as he paced nervously outside the Queen's chambers. This time had seemed forever in coming, and he was about to burst with worry at the outcome.

At last the sound he longed to hear filled the space around him, as the mid-wife emerged from Isabelle's chamber.

"Your Highness, the Queen has delivered a healthy, beautiful daughter," she proudly announced above the cries from the small babe inside.

Byron brimmed with happiness as those around quickly congratulated him on the success of the child's birth. Finally pulling his wits about him, he raised his hand for silence.

"Notify King Malcolm immediately that he, too, has gained a daughter this day. Instruct the Council to administer the betrothal edicts with haste," he commanded. Then, with a wave of his hand he dismissed his audience. "Now, I must see my child."

The new family quickly settled into a routine over the next few days that revolved around the tiny princess. Isabelle spent each afternoon rocking the petite beauty in her cradle and singing to her, as Adeline straightened up the room and prepared for Byron's daily visit when he would take a break from his duties. Isabelle smiled when she heard his knock on the door.

"Enter."

She turned to greet him and was surprised to see he was joined by King Malcolm, and his young son, Roderick.

"Isabelle, my darling. How are you this day?" asked Byron, as he placed a kiss on her forehead.

"I am well, Byron. I see you have brought us visitors."

"Yes," he answered. "All of the necessary edicts have been completed for our little princess' betrothal. Therefore, I thought it would be good for Prince Roderick to meet his future bride."

He leaned over the cradle and lifted the baby into his arms, kissed her delicate forehead, and rocked her gently. "And how is my little Princess?"

Malcolm took in the tender scene, envious of the loving relationship Byron had with his wife, but it mattered not. His goal was never love, it had always been to rule Rookskrieg and now he was one step closer.

"My congratulations to you both," he offered.

"Thank you, King Malcolm," Isabelle responded.

"Will you be having the christening soon?"

"As soon as Isabelle feels up to it," answered Byron.

The young prince had been quietly listening, and he tugged at Malcolm's sleeve. "Papa? What is a christening?"

"It is a special naming ceremony, Roderick."

That made no sense to the boy. "Doesn't the baby have a name?" His face flushed red as the adults laughed at him.

"Of course she does!" Malcolm sarcastically answered.

"What is it?" Roderick ventured.

King Byron answered. "Young Roderick, the baby has been given a name, but to speak it aloud invites bad luck. Queen Isabelle and I have waited many years for a child and we do not wish to risk any ill will befalling her. We cannot speak her name until the christening ceremony is completed."

The small boy did not understand this custom, so he opened his mouth to ask another question, but was quickly interrupted by a hasty knock on the chamber door. Before Adeline could get to it, in burst an exuberant Lillith, diving toward Isabelle with a giant hug.

"Oh, dear, dear, Isabelle! I was so excited when I heard the news! A baby for you, at last!" Without a moment's hesitation she leapt from Isabelle's side to Byron's.

"Oh, she is so precious!" she gasped. "May I hold her, Bryon?"

"Of course, Lillith," he answered. It was obvious his sister-in-law's excitement would not be contained, and to deny her would be impossible. He happily handed over his tiny princess. Adeline pulled a chair up next to Isabelle for Lillith, and she quickly sat down. The two sisters' whole attention rested on the baby, as they cooed and played.

Malcolm simply stared for a few moments, allowing the room to settle again. He'd forgotten what a whirlwind of energy the lovely red-head could be.

"Lillith," he began. "I hardly recognized you. You were little more than a child when you left for Elfhame."

"It does seem long ago, but the time has passed quickly," she answered. Then she noticed the young boy hiding behind his father's tall frame. "Is this your son?"

"Yes," he answered as he pulled the boy forward, and gave him a push, indicating he should bow to the woman. "This is Prince Roderick."

"He seems a fine boy," she observed.

"He is now OUR son, too, Lillith," Isabelle declared. "Prince Roderick is betrothed to our little Princess."

"How splendid!" she answered as she returned the baby to her cradle. In spite of Lillith's electric energy, the baby slept peacefully.

"Indeed, but tell me," Isabelle asked. "How is it that Queen Daione has permitted you to leave Elfhame to visit us?"

"This is an official visit, Isabelle," she answered. Lillith stood to her full height, which was not much given her slight frame, but her bearing revealed all the power she had acquired since her indoctrination into the fairylands of Elfhame. "The Fairy Queen has instructed me to bestow one special gift upon your child. You must help me decide what it shall be. Beauty? Grace? Humility?"

Isabelle thought for a moment. "This is not an easy decision."

"It does not have to be made this very moment," answered Lillith. "I will be staying for a few days."

"I'm so glad. I have missed you, Lillith."

Byron knew the words were sincere. As a young girl, Isabelle had been close with her sisters, and the rifts that had been created in their kingdom with the loss of her sisters weighed heavily on her gentle heart. "Yes, Isabelle has..."

His words were cut short as the door to Isabelle's chamber slammed open, and a furious purple whirlwind cut through the chamber laying a path to the cradle of the new Princess. The stunned group watched in awe as the whirlwind dissolved into a purple mist. As the fog faded, Elspeth appeared in all her majesty, resting lightly on the silver staff she bore, with Irwing at her side. A second later, a silver-haired boy stepped from behind, but he clung cautiously to her hand.

Elspeth held Isabelle's gaze for a moment, before she pulled young Ossian forward to look upon the sleeping baby. He studied the bundle of pink and white light. He had never seen anything so bright and beautiful. He looked back up at his mother and she smiled tenderly. As the moment ended, she set about her mission.

"How quaint!" she directed her comments to King Byron. "A family reunion, though my invitation appears to have been lost."

Then her attention turned to Isabelle. "But I knew YOU would be expecting me."

Isabelle was frozen in fear.

"You were not invited to our home," snapped Byron.

"I beg to differ," snarled Elspeth. "Not only was I invited, your Queen has promised the joining of our realms through the betrothal of your daughter to my son, Ossian."

She paused for effect, watching the reactions of each one in turn. Byron's shock, Malcolm's anger, and Isabelle's horror... Dear Isabelle, who was begging with her eyes for Elspeth to leave, and when she saw that Elspeth would not waver, her eyes turned to beg Byron for forgiveness. It was a moment Elspeth savored.

"Byron... Please... I'm sorry," she cried. "I was desperate."

"Silence," he commanded, as he turned to his sister-in-law. "Leave now, Elspeth."

She ignored him, continuing her diatribe. "When the betrothal to Jethart's son has been honored and the edicts completed, King Byron."

"The edicts have been completed," he retorted. "The Princess is betrothed to Malcolm's son, Prince Roderick. Now, leave!"

Elspeth glared at Malcolm and his young son in turn. Roderick thought her dark eyes would bore clear through him. He sank behind his father in fear.

Noting his fear, Elspeth softened her gaze, and turned her attention back to Byron.

"You promised..." she began.

"I promised nothing to you," he growled. "And whatever was promised by my wife was not hers to offer." Byron drew his sword in a threatening manner, and Malcolm did the same. "I am telling you for the last time to leave this realm."

Elspeth quaked with anger at Byron's daring. She took a few moments to recompose herself. She refused to let Byron have the upper hand.

"If that's the way it must be, then I shall leave as you request, King Byron." She made a mockery of bowing to him. "But first, allow me to bestow a gift on the Princess Ealasaid…"

The group gasped, horrified that Elspeth had dared to speak the babe's name. Lillith was the first to confront her.

"NO! Why did you speak her name? You know it bodes evil!"

"Do I?" answered Elspeth, venom dripping from her words. "Did you really think I would be happy that you should give this child my middle name rather than honoring the betrothal? I gave you this life, and I shall take it back." She glared at each in turn, finally resting her gaze on Malcolm. "Just as you have taken what I deemed most precious!"

"NO!" Isabelle screamed, but she was too late. Elspeth's magic was already in motion. The orb of her staff glowed brightly and several small purple whirlwinds bounced about the room, preventing any of them from stopping her. She began to weave runes in the air as she worked her spell.

"Princess Ealasaid, so beautiful and small, I gave you your first gift, most precious of all. Lifeblood and being, a future so dear, and now another gift in the future near. Before the day you can be wed, those who love you shall find you dead. You'll pierce your hand on a spindle of gold, and suddenly you will grow old. As death encompasses your last heartbeat, your final fate shall you meet."

As Elspeth finished her spell, Isabelle grabbed the baby and hugged her to her chest. Byron dived toward Elspeth with his sword, but Elspeth just laughed. With a sweep of her robes, she and her entourage disappeared in a purple mist.

Malcolm could feel the life ebbing from the room with Elspeth's disappearance. Isabelle was sobbing uncontrollably and Byron could hardly breathe, but he pulled Isabelle and the baby into his arms, attempting to console his wife.

"All is well, Isabelle. She is gone. Our child is no longer in danger." But Lillith knew this was not true. She knew the gravity of what had just transpired in the Queen's chamber.

"You are wrong, King Byron. Elspeth's power is great."

"What can we do?" Byron sighed. "We could not bear to lose Ealasaid. She is our only child, and we can have no other."

"Forgive me, my husband," Isabelle cried.

"What's done is done," he quietly answered.

"I have yet to bestow my gift on the Princess," Lillith offered. "Now we know what that gift must be. The Dark Queen has left us but one choice… to wish away Ealasaid's death."

A glimmer of hope broke through the tears on Isabelle's face. "Can you save her, Lillith? Can you rid my child of this death wish?"

"I can change the spell, but I cannot remove it. As I said, Elspeth's magic is strong."

"Please," begged Byron. "Do what you can!"

Lillith took a moment to gather her energy around her, then she took the small babe from Isabelle and laid her back in her cradle. She focused intently with arms outstretched, pulling a brilliant blue light into her space as she began her spell.

"Princess Ealasaid, frail and small, I'll protect you from death's call. Instead of death, I give you peace. Quiet slumber and reposed sleep, where you will rest in dreams of bliss until awakened by true love's kiss."

As she finished her spell the blue light around her fell in sprinkles of fairy dust across the baby. All could only wait to see if the evil spell had been broken.

With Lillith's spell in place, it was now Byron's job to do what he could to protect his child. He strode to the door and shouted an order to the guards in the hallway. "Destroy all of the spindles in the realm! Do it this very day... at once!"

As the guards scrambled to fulfill his command, he returned to the cradle and picked up Ealasaid. "I shall do everything in my power to protect you, my little Princess."

"There is one more thing," Lillith said, "She should be christened as soon as possible to ward off any further evil."

"Yes, you are correct, Lillith." He handed the baby to Lillith, and nodded for Malcolm to join him. "I shall call the Royal Council together at once and summon the Priest. Come to the Great Hall as soon as possible."

Chapter 27
Safe Haven

It was the wee hours of the morning, and a pall hung over Rookskrieg as King Byron placed a rag doll in a satchel and tied it shut. He turned to face Isabelle, who was rocking their baby. She jumped at a knock on the chamber door, and squeezed the sleeping child closer to her. Byron opened the door, allowing Lillith to enter. He handed the satchel to Lillith, then went over and kissed the baby.

"I will protect her with all of the power I have inside of me," Lillith said. "She shall grow to be a beautiful young woman."

Isabelle sobbed. "It is not fair that I must lose my child in order to save her!"

Byron pulled her to him, consoling her.

"Please understand, Isabelle... You must understand. If you had to trust Elspeth's dark magic to conceive this child, then WE must be strong enough to trust in Lillith's good magic to protect her."

Isabelle continued to cry.

"I must go," Lillith stated solemnly. "The Fairies wait to accompany us to safety."

Byron nodded. He reached down lovingly and took the baby from his grieving wife. Handing her to Lillith, he returned to Isabelle's side. Isabelle's wailed as they watched Lillith disappear through the door with their child in her arms.

A few minutes later, Lillith and her bundle emerged from a secret exit at the side of the castle. A dozen fairies hovered in the shadows. As Lillith walked quickly toward the gate, the fairies formed a circle of protection around her. Their bright golden auras provided light to the dark, moonless night. A couple of the fairies, Magenta and Daphne, conversed with Lillith in their tiny musical voices as the group made their way forward.

"What a sad, sad day for good King Byron and his Queen," said Magenta.

"Yes, and what love they have for this little princess to place her in the care of others, knowing they won't see her again until she is grown," Daphne added.

"We must protect her well these coming years, Daphne. And we must be careful in the use of our magic lest we attract Elspeth's watchful eye."

"It's not her EYE I'm worried about at this moment!" Lillith chided. "Will you two hush before you awaken the entire Kingdom?"

The fairies continued through the gate in silence, and turned onto the road. They headed toward the edge of the forest, where darkness finally swallowed them.

Chapter 28
Lessons Begin

His mother no longer allowed him to romp playfully in the courtyard with the goblins, but it didn't make him sad. Nine-year-old Ossian was happy to be allowed into the study of his father, where he practiced magic daily. Today, he was concentrating on making a small imp disappear and reappear, while his friends watched in amazement. He dipped his fingers into a pewter bowl, then threw a bit of white powder to the floor in front of the waiting imp. He was rewarded with a cheer from the others at his success. He repeated the process and the little fellow successfully returned, all agog at the wonder of the magic.

Elspeth watched quietly from the door, her face full of motherly love. As the cheering from the imps subsided, she wound her way through them to Ossian, and placed her hands on his shoulders.

"Ossian, darling! You become more clever with each passing day." She bent and placed a kiss on his forehead, still in wonder at how much the child resembled Jethart. "I wish your father were here to see what a fine young prince you are growing into."

Ossian's chest swelled with pride.

"I have a gift for you, darling," she continued.

The boy responded eagerly. "A gift, Mother? Is it a sword?" He'd been hoping for a real sword to replace the wooden one he used in practice each day with Irwing.

Elspeth laughed softly as she stepped past him and pulled a wrapped parcel out of a nearby cabinet. "No, my darling. It is something much more powerful."

"What could be more powerful than a sword?" he exclaimed. Elspeth smiled knowingly as she handed Ossian the gift. She watched with great anticipation as he opened it, revealing the royal purple cape Jethart had left in her keeping so long ago.

"A cape? Mother, how could this be more powerful than a sword?"

"It's not just any cape, Ossian," she answered, fighting back tears at the memory of that happy day. "It's a very special gift to you from your father. He gave it to me before you were born. He asked that I keep it for you and give it to you when the time was right. I think he knew he would not be here." The tears she had been fighting broke free, gliding down her pale cheeks. Ossian rushed to her, and hugged her tightly.

"Don't cry, Mother. It's a wonderful gift, and I'm glad you saved it for me."

"I love you, Ossian… And so does your father. Never forget that."

As Ossian forged ahead in his magic lessons, all was quiet deep in the forest. Lillith spent her days caring for small Princess Ealasaid. Far from the grown-up lessons Ossian was learning in the Dark Realm, the baby was just learning to walk. Lillith sighed sadly, knowing this moment she enjoyed with the toddling princess was one Isabelle would never experience. She felt badly for her sister. All Isabelle had ever wanted was to be a happy family.

Chapter 29
Becoming a Warrior

Eleven-year-old Prince Roderick was tall for his age. He bore his royalty in his carriage and demeanor as he practiced his swordsmanship in the courtyard of Talonsbay Castle. Other soldiers practiced around him. Sir Lawrence had become his mentor in the arts of war, and his greatest confidant. Roderick stopped for a moment as the older soldier approached.

"Very good, my Prince. Next, we shall work on tilting."

"When can I start going out with the soldiers, Sir Lawrence?"

"What is your hurry?" Lawrence chuckled.

"I want to win a great battle and be a hero, just like my Father!"

"And who would you defeat, young Prince? The realms are peaceful, save for the black mists ruled by the Dark Queen."

"My Father says she is no threat – just a weak woman."

"Women are far stronger than the King gives them credit for. *I* would not want to reckon with a vengeful sorceress."

Lawrence left Roderick to contemplate his words.

Chapter 30
Transformation

Time passed quickly behind the walls of Dubh Rathgart. Elspeth could hardly believe her son was now thirteen. He grew stronger each day, and today she was pushing him to even greater strength.

"I cannot do it, Mother!" he complained. "It is too hard!"

"No!" she admonished him. "You can do it, darling. You must remember what I taught you about focus." She took his hands in her own, and stared intently into his eyes. "Now. I want you to concentrate and focus with me."

She closed her eyes, and the teen followed suit. As they stood with their hands locked a whirlwind, small at first, began to encircle them. As they continued their concentration it grew in size and momentum until the pair was engulfed. The imps and goblins watching from the corners began to screech as the room shuddered under the force of the powerful magic. They ran for cover as jars and bottles crashed to the floor. Suddenly the room was illuminated in a bright flash, then everything was eerily silent. Elspeth stood alone in the center of the room, disheveled by the power of the whirlwind that had been created. She turned at the sound of a small owl that hooted from a high shelf behind her. "Woooo…" it sang.

She clapped her hands in glee.

"Ossian! You've done it. You've done it!"

The imps and goblins came out from their hiding places and joined in her cheering. Ossian joined in their celebration as he spread his wings and swooped about the room, at last coming to rest on his Mother's shoulder.

She smiled in admiration as she smoothed his ruffled feathers. "Well done, my son," she complimented. "Soon you will be ready to join our search for your little princess, Ealasaid. We shall rightfully reclaim what is ours."

Elspeth had been searching, but not far enough. Deep in the forest, Lillith watched from a cottage window as Princess Ealasaid played tag with a group of fairies that fluttered around her. Just five years old, she was so innocent dragging her rag doll behind her. Lillith pondered the memory of that day when King Byron had handed over Ealasaid and her doll to the care of the fairies, and she wondered how much longer their peaceful existence in the forest would last.

Chapter 31
The Sorcerer Apprentice

Eight years after Princess Ealasaid was christened, sixteen-year-old Ossian stood in the courtyard of Dubh Rathgart, holding his mother's staff. Each day he pushed himself to greater feats of magic. And each day his resolve to avenge his father's death grew stronger. He carefully balanced on the balcony ledge, illuminated by the brightness of the full moon, and he raised the staff high. The orb began to glow, ever brighter, as he raised his other hand and stood, arms outstretched to the heavens. A great wind threatened to lift him off the ground.

His prolonged shout of triumph echoed as sparks exploded from the orb and rained down over his body. In an instant, a vacuum formed, sucking at the spark-filled air until all that remained was the staff. It clattered to the ground, the orb now dim. Ossian was nowhere to be found.

In the meantime, eight-year-old Ealasaid sat at the dining table in the forest cottage, a book open before her. Lillith sat beside her, clearly teaching her to read. Ealasaid's finger ran along a line in the book as she struggled to make out a word. Finally succeeding, she looked toward Lillith, who laughed and hugged her young pupil.

Ealasaid was glad her aunt was teaching her to read. Even though the fairies were lots of fun to play with, she grew lonely sometimes. She was never allowed far from the cottage, and she yearned to know what the rest of the world was like.

Chapter 32
Lessons in Vengeance

It had been twelve years since the fateful day of Princess Ealasaid's christening. But the memory of the magnificent brightness that surrounded the baby, and his mother's promise of her betrothal weighed heavily on Ossian's mind this day. He was now twenty years old, and anxious to find the Princess and take his rightful place as ruler of the Dark Realm.

All of this thinking did not dull his reactions, though, and he let loose the blade of his father's great sword as Irwing and a band of goblins attacked him from behind. Still, he tired of these daily lessons. He was ready for a real battle.

"Very good, Ossian," Irwing barked. "You fight well. Your father would be proud."

Ossian turned his father's sword in his hands, studying the mighty weapon. "I must fight well, Irwing," he answered. "It is my destiny to avenge my Mother's honor and to destroy those who stole my Father from us."

"And your princess," the goblin added.

"Yes. And my princess. I wonder what she is like?"

Ossian fell in beside the goblin as he made his way into the fortress' side entrance. "Mother says she was born especially for me. What does she mean by that, Irwing?"

"It was our Queen's magic that conceived the Princess Ealasaid. She was meant to be yours from that moment on, but King Byron refused to honor the betrothal. He promised her to King Malcolm's son instead."

Ossian's face darkened at the mention of the hated King. He couldn't keep the venomous tone from his voice. "He deserves to die for the trespasses he has committed against our family. Someday I will kill him."

"Yes," concurred Irwing. "And his son."

Chapter 33
Illusion and Innocence

Six years older, Roderick was now allowed to lead patrols with the soldiers in the land of Talonsbay. Lawrence sat with Roderick in a farmyard, apart from the small band of soldiers they were commanding. The soldiers accosted the farmer and made crude remarks to his wife. They stole the bread and pies that were cooling on the window ledge of the small cottage. Roderick looked on until he had his fill.

"These men have no honor," he spat.

"I recall when you couldn't wait to accompany them," Lawrence replied.

"Why does my father allow such behavior in his ranks, Lawrence?"

"Begging your pardon, Prince, but it has been my observation that the King of Talonsbay cares little about anything except his own desires."

Offended, Roderick suddenly stood, towering over Lawrence.

"How dare you speak thus? My father is a hero. He saved our realm from the Dark King."

"Yes, so the story goes." Lawrence's tone was sarcastic. He rose and moved to mount his horse, but Roderick grabbed his arm.

"What do you mean by that, Lawrence?"

"Nothing, my Prince. I mean nothing by it." Lawrence looked Roderick squarely in the eye. "I served at your father's side in that battle. I witnessed his 'great' deeds. Perhaps someday I will tell you about them."

Yanking his arm away, the old soldier ordered the others to mount up. He got on his horse and urged it forward, leaving Roderick staring after him.

Meanwhile, twelve-year-old Ealasaid sat in a chair by the fireplace in Lillith's cottage, reading one of her cherished books. Her aunt sat in a chair across from her, sewing. As Ealasaid finished the last page, she closed the book and hugged it to her chest, a dreamy look in her eye.

"Oh, Aunt Lillith! Wouldn't it be wonderful?"

"Wouldn't what be wonderful, dear?"

Still hugging the book, Ealasaid stood and twirled. "To be loved by a handsome prince and live in a large castle with LOTS and LOTS of people!"

Lillith looked down at her sewing, trying to hide her sly smile. Ealasaid breathed a romantic sigh as she sank back into the chair by the hearth. A couple of fairies who were hiding and playing around the hearth peeked out and giggled at the love-struck girl.

"Perhaps, Ealasaid," Lillith replied. "But life in a castle is not always so perfect as it seems, and not every prince is to be coveted."

"But my prince would be wonderful, Aunt Lillith. He would fall deeply in love with me the first time we met."

Another dreamy sigh from the young princess drew a laugh from Lillith.

"I'm sure a prince would fall in love with you, my dear. Truly, madly, deeply in love with you."

Lillith turned her attention back to her sewing. Ealasaid opened the book to read the story over again. One of the fairies from the mantle fluttered over and sat on Ealasaid's shoulder, to read along.

Chapter 34
The Rightful Heir

Dark skies marked the day of Ossian's twenty-fourth birthday. The darkness only added to the ambience of the ceremony about to take place. Ossian rocked on his heels at the entrance to the Great Hall and fidgeted with his long purple cape as he waited for the signal from his mother.

At the far end of the room, standing before the black marble throne, Elspeth's heart swelled with pride. She raised the silver crown she held in her hands and tipped it towards Ossian ever so slightly.

He bowed lowly to his mother, his Queen, and waited for the flare of the trumpets. As the music began he rose and started his march to the throne with slow, deliberate steps. He looked neither left, nor right, at the line of imps and goblins bearing arms that stood at attention until his passing, who then bowed deeply in respect. Finally reaching the dais, Ossian knelt before his mother. She stepped down to the floor where he waited, and reverently placed Jethart's former crown upon his head. Ossian rose, taking her hand, and together they climbed the dais and turned to face their loyal subjects.

Irwing rapped his staff three times on the floor, and made a proclamation. "All hail the Crown Prince, Ossian!"

The creatures of the realm raised their weapons in Ossian's honor and cheered him heartily. Ossian stood proudly before them, reveling in this new chapter of his life. The time had finally come for a marriage, and a reckoning.

But two weeks later, all was not going as smoothly as the coronation had. Elspeth was in a rage as she paced back and forth in Ossian's chamber. Ossian was just as frustrated, but he tried his best not to show it.

"Two weeks since your coronation and still she eludes our grasp!" she fumed. "This will NOT do, Ossian!"

"I'm sorry, Mother."

"Sorry? She is YOUR intended. YOUR rightful wife!"

"I know, Mother," he sighed. "And tomorrow the search shall continue. We will not stop until she is found."

Suddenly Elspeth stopped her pacing and stared at Ossian through narrowed eyes.

"What is it?" he asked.

"Tomorrow she shall be found."

"You are certain?"

"Yes," she hissed. "It is almost time for the betrothal to be sealed. She MUST be found. Now, you must rest, for there will be much work to do tomorrow." She immediately headed to the door. "Good night, Ossian. Sleep well."

Ossian stared after her. His Mother divined something she was not telling.

Chapter 35
A Happy Journey

Malcolm stood at the window of a stateroom in Talonsbay Castle, reading a letter. Twenty-two-year-old Roderick waited patiently at his side. When finished reading, Malcolm folded the letter.

"What news from King Byron, Father?" Roderick asked.

"He sends for you…"

"Me? Why?"

"It is time for your betrothal to Princess Ealasaid to be sealed. Byron asks that you bring her from her place of hiding and deliver her safely to his castle. You will then remain there until you two are wed."

Roderick was not sure he bought into the plan. "I don't know where she is!" he blurted. "Besides, maybe I don't want to marry her. She could be as ugly as a crow for all I know!"

King Malcolm chuckled. "You have no fears there, my son. She was blessed with beauty." His face suddenly turned serious. "Besides, I have waited many years to join the lands of Rookskrieg with mine. There can be no more delays… or disruptions!" Roderick stepped back as the King pounded his fist on a nearby desk. "I will not tolerate them!"

Roderick was startled by his father's outburst. Recovering his composure, Malcolm handed his son the folded letter as he continued. "This letter provides all the information you need to find Ealasaid. Go... make preparations. You must leave early in the morning."

"Yes, Sir," Roderick replied. With a slight bow, he left the room.

The next day, Prince Roderick arrived at the cottage, which was in a state of heightened activity as the Princess was preparing for her journey. When Ealasaid and Roderick met, he was so taken aback by her beauty that he was speechless. Ealasaid, having never met a young man before, let alone a handsome prince, was struck just as speechless. They stood in awkward silence as a servant saddled the horses and helped Lillith and the fairies lash Ealasaid's belongings to the back of a pack horse.

A short time later, the entourage was sauntering slowly down the road. They paid no attention to the owl that flew above them from branch to branch. Roderick moved his horse alongside Ealasaid's. She glanced sideways through her long, dark lashes.

"I suppose you are excited to be returning to your castle?" Roderick finally offered.

"I'm not really sure how I feel. I've never been there," Ealasaid replied.

"Of course you have," Roderick stated.

The princess shifted uncomfortably in her saddle. "Well, I suppose you are correct, but I don't remember it."

"I guess you were just a baby when you left. I remember the day of your christening, though." Roderick shuddered.

The owl circled overhead then flew closer to the couple, as if to eavesdrop.

"My father and I were visiting," Roderick continued. "I don't recall why, but we were talking with Lillith and then suddenly, the Dark Queen entered the room. Her presence threw a pall over the ceremony. I remember thinking, though, that she was more… attractive… than I expected. I didn't understand why she was so angry at the time, but now I do. She was jealous of you, Princess… jealous of your unsurpassed beauty."

Ealasaid blushed. In the trees above, the owl let out a mournful screech. Roderick turned and watched as it quickly flew away.

He looked back at Ealasaid, who smiled, clearly enchanted with her betrothed. He returned her smile.

Back at Dubh Rathgart, Elspeth was tending to her lavender roses. She looked up as an owl approached. Hovering before her, the bird dissolved into a purple mist, which transformed into Ossian.

"I have found her, Mother!" he cried.

"Are you certain?" Elspeth removed her gardening gloves and took her son by the shoulders.

"Yes," Ossian replied. "Prince Roderick is escorting her to King Byron's castle in Rookskrieg. Shall I go and take her from him and bring her here?" His eyes were bright at the prospect.

"No… No, Ossian." The Dark Prince's countenance dropped at his mother's reprimand. "It is not enough to just bring her here. Prince Roderick must be destroyed, as well, or he will destroy us."

As she spoke, Elspeth ripped a rose from a nearby bush and crushed it. The thorns dug into her flesh and caused her to bleed. "And when Prince Roderick is dead and the Princess is in our hands, then I will have succeeded in hurting King Malcolm as deeply as he has hurt us." Blood trailed off her hand onto the ground.

Chapter 36
A Family United

A pair of white owls made a large lazy circle about the courtyard of Rookskrieg Castle, as they watched over the bustle of activity below. Finally, the pair came to rest on the window ledge of a room high in one of the castle's great turrets.

Inside the room a family reunion was taking place. King Byron's aged face was bright with happiness as he watched Queen Isabelle hug Ealasaid tightly. "I can hardly believe this is the same small babe I held in my arms," she cried.

Ealasaid blushed as she looked back at Lillith and Adeline standing behind her. She'd only just learned her parents were alive. She hardly knew how to react to their loving welcome. They were strangers to her, and she'd been told repeatedly by Lillith to stay away from strangers. She felt awkward.

Byron stepped forward and took his daughter's hands into his own. "She has grown into a beautiful young woman, just as you promised, Lillith. Come, Isabelle. Let us leave them to settle in while we prepare to greet our guests." He placed a kiss on Ealasaid's cheek, just as pink and dainty as he remembered, then took Isabelle's hand and escorted her from the room.

Ealasaid watched their retreat, and the flurry of activity as Lillith and Adeline began to unpack her trunk. She knew she should probably help, but the sunbeams sliding through the window called to her. She languidly strolled to the window, but stopped short as she noticed the two white owls sitting on the ledge. "How strange!" she remarked.

"What's that, dear?" Lillith asked absently as she went about her tasks.

"The birds on the window ledge."

Lillith's eyes met Adeline's, and the servant quickly stepped to the window and shooed the birds away. She locked the shutters and checked them twice. "That's better. We can't be too careful."

"This is all so silly!" whined Ealasaid. "I don't understand what you think the Dark Queen has to do with me. And I don't understand all of this secrecy."

Lillith went to her side, and took her hand. "Ealasaid, your very existence has depended on it. The Dark Queen has…"

"Stop it! Please." Ealasaid yanked her hand from Lillith's grasp. "I don't want to hear any more. Yesterday, I lived a quiet life in the woods, and today I am thrust into a new life that I don't understand." She threw herself upon the bed, as total misery threatened to overtake her.

"But Ealasaid, you need…"

"She needs to have a few minutes to herself," offered Adeline. She knew arguing with the girl at this moment would not help. "Come, Lillith. Let us retrieve the rest of the Princess' things." She ushered Lillith to the door. "Bolt the door behind us, Princess. We'll return shortly."

With a sigh, Ealasaid forced herself from the bed and bolted the door behind them, as instructed. She leaned against the heavy door for a few moments, reveling in her first minutes of total peace since this whole ordeal had begun with the arrival of Roderick. Thinking of him brought a smile back to her face. He was everything she had imagined a handsome prince would be. When she at last turned away from the door, she was shocked to find a man standing in the center of her room. It was all she could do to stifle a scream that threatened to escape.

"Who are you?" she finally asked, taking in his odd appearance. A purple hooded cloak covered his otherwise-black garb. He dropped the hood to reveal pale skin and silvery hair that stuck out like feathers. She had never seen anyone like him, yet there was something oddly familiar about him.

"I am Ossian." He bowed. "Your intended."

"I am betrothed to Prince Roderick," she answered tentatively. "I don't know you."

"You didn't know him yesterday, either. Besides, do you believe everything they tell you?"

She could tell he meant Lillith and Adeline. "Shouldn't I?" she countered.

"They have deceived others. Why not you, too?" He paused for a moment, gauging her reaction. "They don't want you to know about me. They conspire to keep us apart, Ealasaid."

She shook her head. "No. I don't believe you. You try to trick me, Sir."

"Come with me, Ealasaid," he coaxed as he took a step forward. "I'll take you to the woods where we can live, hidden away from the deceitful people of this world." He placed a hand on her waist and tried to pull her into his embrace, just as he had imagined he would a thousand times before, but she fought his grasp.

"NO! Get away from me! I don't know you."

"Ealasaid…" he whispered, trying to gain her confidence.

"Go away!" she continued. "DON'T TOUCH ME!"

Angered and insulted by her rejection, he pushed her away. "You shall soon wish you went with me!" he threatened. "Nothing but death awaits you in this castle."

Ealasaid watched in horror as he dissolved into a purple whirlwind before her eyes. As the whirlwind disappeared into the ceiling of her chamber, she rushed to the bed and threw herself upon it, bursting into tears. She cried hard into the pillows, not knowing how much more she could take this day. She raised her head from the pillow as she heard the latch on the door click. She sat up expecting Lillith and Adeline. She watched in surprise as an old woman shuffled into her room, carrying a golden staff in her hand. She scooted to the edge of the bed and wiped at the tears on her face. She had never seen such a staff before. She stared at it for a moment, then at the old woman. "Who are you?" she asked.

"I thought I heard someone crying. And, I might ask you the same question."

"My name is Ealasaid."

"Ah," the old woman answered knowingly. "King Byron's daughter. Has time passed so quickly? Why are you crying, child?"

"There was a strange man here. He frightened me," she confessed.

"A stranger? Here?" She looked about the room. "Let's be safe then, shall we? Hold this while I bolt the door."

Ealasaid happily received the staff, anxious to get a closer look at it. "I thought I had locked the door," she told the old woman, who shuffled across the room. "I don't know how he got in here."

"This old castle has many secret passages," the old hag offered. "It's hard to say how he came to be here, but no one can enter now."

"What is this?" Ealasaid asked, her full attention on the staff now that she knew the door was locked.

"It's a spindle, child. Have you never seen one?"

"No," Ealasaid answered. "What do you do with it?"

"It's used to spin thread." The old woman sat herself down heavily beside the Princess on the bed. "Place the fingers of your other hand on the point at the top," she instructed. "And spin the staff with your lower hand."

Ealasaid attempted to follow her instructions. "Like this?"

As she took her eyes away from the staff to see the old woman's nods, she felt the tip drive into the tender flesh of her fingertip. She gasped and let the spindle fall to the floor with a crash. Blood dripped from her fingers.

"OW!" she exclaimed. Suddenly she felt dizzy. Everything seemed to be turning black around her.

"What's happening to me?" she whispered. "Help me!" she beseeched. She reached out to the old woman, but no one was there. She fell to the floor with a thud. The last thing she heard was evil laughter ringing through the room.

The laughter grew in strength and enthusiasm as the old woman dissolved into a purple mist, then reappeared in the form of Elspeth in all of her royal splendor. Her laughter spent at last, Elspeth stooped over the girl and retrieved the golden spindle. With a wave of her hand, its shape transformed back to that of her silver staff.

"If Ossian cannot have you, then no one can, little Princess." With an evil smile of triumph, Elspeth disappeared in a purple mist.

Lillith could feel a disturbance in the air as she and Adeline approached Ealasaid's room. She dropped the items she carried to the floor, rushing to the Princess' door. She beat on it fiercely.

"Ealasaid! … Open the door, dear. EALASAID!"

But the Princess did not answer. Alarmed, Adeline joined in. "Princess Ealasaid! Let us in!" she cried.

"Something is wrong," Lillith lamented.

"PRINCESS EALASAID!" Adeline threw her body against the door, but the latch would not give.

Lillith pushed her out of the way, withdrawing her wand from deep inside her robes. She waved it at the latch, and the lock gave way under a flash of blue light.

The two women quickly rushed in. They were horrified to find the Princess lying on the floor, her fingers bleeding.

"No!" cried Lillith. "How did this happen?"

"Our beautiful Princess," moaned Adeline, tears spilling from her eyes.

"We've failed. We've failed King Byron."

"He and the Queen will be devastated," agreed Adeline.

Lillith hung her head in sadness for a few minutes. She reflected on everything she had done to save the Princess, only to lose her now. Adeline's weeping affected her, and she knew she could not bear to tell Isabelle this news. Her sister would die of a broken heart, and Lillith knew she could not bear to see her sister cry one more time.

"They must never know," she announced. "We will not tell them."

Adeline looked up in horror. "We have to tell them! This is not something we can hide!"

"No, we cannot hide it," Lillith agreed, "But perhaps they can all sleep with her."

"What are you saying?"

"I shall cast a spell on the castle, Adeline. All will sleep until the evil spell on the Princess is broken."

"But only true love's kiss can break the spell. She has no true love," Adeline sighed.

"You are mistaken," Lillith answered, a knowing smile on her face. "She has Prince Roderick."

"But they only just met!"

"Did you not see the way they looked at each other," she asked. "Now, go to the courtyard and summon the fairies who wait there. I need their help to cast the spell. Hurry!"

Chapter 37
A Wicked Deception

Adeline rushed out of the castle and up a path to where several fairies fluttered and played among the blossoms of the rose garden.

"Good fairies! Please come!" There was urgency in her voice.

"Is it time for the banquet already?" the fairy named Magenta wanted to know.

"I fear not, Miss Magenta. Lillith needs your help. It is a matter of life and death!"

"What does she need?" Magenta asked.

Adeline glanced about, making sure she hadn't been followed. "She will tell you when you arrive. Please! Come quickly with me to Princess Ealasaid's room!"

Adeline turned and scurried back up the path, followed by the group of fairies.

In the hallway of the castle, Elspeth hid in the shadows inside a passageway hall. She peeked out at the sound of approaching footsteps, then pulled herself deeply back into the shadows. She watched Adeline and the fairies go by. Just when she thought they had passed, Magenta flew back and hovered for a moment in front of the recessed area, peering into the darkness. Elspeth held her breath.

"Magenta! Don't dawdle!" Daphne scolded. "Come along!" Her voice echoed through the hall.

Magenta took one last look. "Yes, Daphne," she finally answered.

As Magenta fluttered away to catch up with the rest of the fairies, Elspeth released her breath, then inhaled deeply. After a few moments, she heard footsteps again, the heavy footsteps of a man. She peeked around the wall in time to see Prince Roderick approaching. He was alone, and humming to himself.

Staying hidden in the shadows, Elspeth held her staff before her and closed her eyes. She began to form runes in the air. A light breeze surrounded her, and suddenly she transformed into Princess Ealasaid.

Noticing some commotion in the area where Elspeth was, Roderick walked in her direction, a look of curiosity on his face. Before he reached the recess, Elspeth, appearing as Ealasaid, jumped into his path. A long hooded cloak covered her dress.

"My Prince!" she cried. "You must come at once! Please! Hurry!"

Roderick finally found his voice. "Ealasaid! What's wrong?" He looked around behind her. "Where did you come from?"

"There's no time!" she insisted. "Please! We must hurry!"

She grabbed Roderick's hand and began to drag him down the passage.

"Princess!" he huffed as they ran. "Slow down! What's wrong? Where are we going?"

They ran to the end of the passage and down a dark stairway to a small exterior door located at the bottom of the steps. The door was a secret passage into and out of the castle.

Elspeth/Ealasaid pushed the door open and led the way out. Two castle guards stood nearby. She ducked, pulling Roderick down beside her, hiding behind a wooden rain barrel.

"Ealasaid, if we…" Elspeth/Ealasaid clapped her hand over Roderick's mouth. Putting her finger to her lips, she took him by the hand. He looked at her curiously, but allowed her to drag him across the courtyard. They hid behind barrels, wagons, and other items as they made their way toward the castle gate. They were able to escape the notice of the guards, and finally ran through the gate to the road outside the castle walls. A horse stood in the middle of the road, already saddled and ready to ride.

"Quickly, dear Roderick! We must escape!"

"Escape?" Roderick was confused. "What are we escaping from?"

"Please… We must leave NOW! Mount the horse and I will explain on the way!" Elspeth/Ealasaid's tone was persuasive. Though troubled, Roderick helped her mount the horse, and he climbed into the saddle behind her. Prodding the horse with his heels, they took off swiftly.

Twenty minutes later, as they made their way up the road, Elspeth/Ealasaid and Roderick slowed their pace. Rookskrieg Castle was barely visible in the distance. Finally, Roderick stopped and climbed down from the horse. Elspeth/Ealasaid landed with a slight bounce as Roderick helped her down. Facing her, he took her hands and looked into her eyes.

"Now, love, you know I would do anything for you, but would you please explain?"

"Certainly, my Prince…"

Elspeth/Ealasaid stepped back and reached under her cloak, pulling out her staff. Holding it out, her form began to dissolve into Elspeth before the Prince's eyes.

"You witch!" he exclaimed. "What is…"

Before he could finish his sentence, he was descended upon by several imps and goblins that had been hiding along the roadside. They pulled him down and bound him with rope. As they did, he could hear the Dark Queen's evil laugh.

Back at Rookskrieg Castle, there was a bustle of activity in the hall as servants set out food, preparing for the magnificent homecoming banquet. The fairies fluttered above as King Byron and Queen Isabelle welcomed their guests. Fairy dust streaks rained down upon the throng. Soon, people began to swoon, and fall into a deep sleep. The fairies flew out a window and into a courtyard, sprinkling their dust as they went.

Chapter 38
Learning the Truth

Later that day, at Dubh Rathgart, Roderick found himself chained to a wall in a dungeon. Elspeth stood before him, holding her staff. Two armed imps stood guard just outside the cell door.

"Well, well… A royal guest in my home," Elspeth taunted.

She dropped to her knees, bowing low before him.

"Welcome, Your Highness," she continued.

"Where is Ealasaid?" Roderick demanded. "What have you done with her, you evil witch?"

Elspeth feigned shock. "Evil, is it? What know you of evil, Prince?" She rose and looked suddenly thoughtful.

"Tell me, why is it we arrange marriages?"

Despite his anger, Roderick could not hide his puzzlement.

"I should have been your mother. Did you know that?" Elspeth continued.

Roderick's eyes grew wide. His expression was not lost on the Dark Queen. She stepped close to him. "Yes, it's true. I'll wager that your father never told you that he and I were to be married, did he?"

Ossian appeared in the doorway, unnoticed by Elspeth and Roderick. Ossian stood silently, taking in the interaction between his mother and the captured Prince.

"STILL you make no answer?!" Elspeth spat. Calming herself, she continued. "I suppose it comes as a shock. But there is more you need to know. ... You seem a nice young man. Malcolm must not have been the one to raise you."

"How dare you defile my father in this manner!" Malcolm shouted.

"Ah! Finally he speaks! Tell me, Roderick... Did your father ever... taunt... your mother? Raise a hand to her, even?"

"I never knew my mother. She died when I was young."

"Oh... I am sorry." Elspeth's tone was almost sincere. "How did she die?"

"Of a fever," the Prince replied.

"A fever? One that caused her to FALL down the steps, perhaps?"

"What nonsense do you speak?" Roderick demanded.

Elspeth's voice turned to velvet. "Observe, Prince..." She lifted her staff so that the orb was level with Roderick's eyes. The orb began to glow. A purple mist filled the inside, then slowly dissipated as a scene began to form.

Two figures stood at the top of the staircase, arguing. One of the figures was King Malcolm. Across from him was a beautiful young woman – Roderick's mother, Queen Mary.

Roderick was transfixed as the argument, which could only be seen, not heard, grew more heated. Suddenly, Malcolm slapped Mary. She tried to back away from him, fear in her eyes. Malcolm grabbed her by the shoulders and threw her down the long stone staircase. She landed at the bottom, and lay completely still.

"This is a lie! A trick of your evil magic!" Roderick was shaken.

"NO!" Elspeth shouted. "NO lie… NO trick!"

Roderick looked again into the orb. He saw his mother lying on her bed, her quiet face battered and bruised, blood trickling from her mouth. As he watched, he saw a young boy looking at her. The sadness in the boy's face filled the orb as tears began to fall from his eyes. As the image faded, Roderick's eyes glistened with sadness. The realization of the truth began to set in. Elspeth ran a finger down his cheek.

"You have witnessed the truth." Her voice was hushed. "The EVIL truth about your father."

"My mother…"

"And my Jethart," Elspeth replied. "Do you know how my husband died?"

Roderick turned his face away, all too aware of the triumphant defeat of the Dark King at the hands of his father.

"Why yes," Elspeth continued. "I can see that you do. But no doubt your version of the story and mine would differ greatly."

"My father is a hero!" Roderick was trying to convince himself.

"The truth must be difficult for you, child. Do you know how difficult it has been for my son to grow up without a father?"

Ossian still stood in the doorway, unnoticed. At his mother's words, his expression hardened. He set his jaw, but remained silent.

Elspeth stood before a clearly distraught Roderick. "The people feared my Jethart... Considered him evil, a King of Darkness." She paused. "But they did not know him."

Elspeth turned her back on Roderick, tears forming in her eyes.

"Not as I did," she continued. When her composure returned, Elspeth turned to face Roderick again.

"Your father arrived with his army. Somehow, they had found us. Ossian was not yet born." The Queen began to pace, too absorbed to notice her son in the doorway.

"Do you know what he came for?"

Without replying, Roderick stared defiantly at his captor.

"He came to murder my husband... the husband who rescued me at the marriage altar from the evil grip of your father. Malcolm was intent on having his vengeance for the wounding of his pride. And on reclaiming his 'property...' Me... And my father's lands. I was nothing more to him than a dowry. As soon as he saw that I was with child, your LOVING father threw me out, leaving me to face the world – to raise my son – alone."

She stopped and faced Roderick squarely. "What think you of evil, now, young Roderick?"

"I think you seek the same vengeance that you claim makes my father an evil man!"

Elspeth was taken aback at the force of the young man's words. She turned away from him as Jethart's voice echoed in her mind. *"Once you step upon the path of vengeance, your destiny is sealed. The pain you visit on others shall revisit you a thousand-fold..."*

She closed her eyes and shook her head slightly to clear her mind of the memory.

"Well... perhaps it is all a matter of perspective, then, isn't it?" she said quietly.

Ossian finally stepped into the cell. "Enough of this!" he shouted.

Startled, Elspeth whirled toward him.

"Ossian! How long have you been...?"

"TOO long!" Ossian interrupted. "This drivel is pointless!"

He stepped between his mother and Roderick, facing the prince, and slowly drew his sword, nothing but hatred in his eyes.

"I'll draw your final blood..." he threatened Roderick. "I am going to kill you, Your Highness, in the same manner that your father MURDERED my own! Vengeance SHALL be loosed upon the wicked!"

He was in Roderick's face. An evil smile crossed his lips as he stared the son of Malcolm down.

"Burn in the flames of hell, you royal scum!"

Elspeth was frozen in shock, seeing her son with new eyes. As he raised his sword to deliver the death blow, her eyes grew wide. She stepped quickly toward him.

"OSSIAN!" Her voice was commanding.

Ossian brought the sword down just short of plunging it into Roderick's heart. Elspeth closed her eyes. As Ossian whirled to face her, Elspeth shrank from his crazed expression.

"WHAT IS IT?" Ossian confronted his mother.

"Not yet," she pleaded. "I... I am not ready to kill him yet."

"NOT READY? This is a moment we have awaited for years. How could you not be ready?" Ossian tried to push her out of the way. "Stand aside, Mother! Do not try to deny me this justice!"

"Ossian... Where is the justice in killing a defenseless man?"

"You grow weak, Mother. I tire of this game."

Elspeth looked from her son to Roderick.

Roderick finally spoke up. "Look... If you're going to kill me, why don't you just do it?"

Elspeth continued to look at the two princes, panic in her eyes. Roderick noticed her expression. Ossian stepped up to Roderick and held his sword against the prisoner's throat.

"Shut up, you fool! I shall relish granting your death wish!"

Once again, he raised his sword. This time, Elspeth ran to her son and grabbed his arm before the sword could penetrate. The blade clattered to the floor.

"MOTHER! WHAT ARE YOU DOING?"

"No, Ossian! Not now... not in this way!"

"But..." Ossian was incredulous.

"LEAVE US! IMMEDIATELY!" the Dark Queen commanded.

Glaring at her, Ossian retrieved his sword, turned on his heel, and left the cell.

"Thank you." Roderick's words were genuine.

"Do not become overconfident, Prince. Your stay of execution is only temporary."

"I don't think so. Otherwise, you would have allowed him to kill me." Roderick hesitated, not sure of how the Queen would react to his words. "You don't want this," he finally ventured. "I see it in your eyes, hear it in your voice... Free me. Tell me where you have taken Ealasaid. I promise no punishment will come to you if you do as I ask."

"Malcolm will..."

"...will never have to know!" the Prince interrupted. "Please! End this wicked game now. Ealasaid and I will..."

"It's too late." Elspeth's eyes betrayed her fear.

"NO! It's not too late!" cried Roderick.

"You do not understand," the Queen said darkly. "Even if I wished to change the course of events, it is all too late. She is dead."

"WHAT?" Roderick strained against the chains.

"The Princess... Ealasaid... she is dead." Elspeth turned on her heel. "I must take my leave now." Her tone was earnest. As she hurried from the cell, a shaken Roderick tried to absorb her words.

A few minutes later, Elspeth ran up the last three steps of a staircase that led to a circular hallway. She ran to a door, pushed it open, and entered her room. The door slammed behind her.

Chapter 39
A Dark Battle

The blackness in his heart carried Ossian quickly across the courtyard of Dubh Rathgart. It burned with one purpose. "IRWING!" he shouted. "IRWING? Where are you?"

The goblin scurried from the dark to appear at his Prince's side. "I am here, Prince Ossian."

Ossian fastened the tie on his cape, and pulled on his heavy leather gloves as he spoke. "My mother grows weak, Irwing. I think she needs to be reminded of her past."

"Reminded of her past? What are you saying? She lives with her memories every day." Irwing studied Ossian's dark countenance. "Ossian? What has happened?"

Ossian threw his hands up in exasperation. "I don't understand, Irwing," he scowled. "She has spent years plotting her revenge on King Malcolm, and now that she holds his son, she hesitates. She refuses to allow me to kill that villain!"

"She is a wise and powerful Queen, Ossian," the goblin offered. "I'm sure she has good reason."

"Perhaps she thinks she does, but..." Ossian stopped his words as a new realization crossed his mind. "But of course she does!" he exclaimed. "How could I not see it? To simply kill the son is not enough. Gather a patrol, Irwing. QUICKLY!"

"A patrol? For what, my Prince?"

A sinister grimace crossed Ossian's face. "To retrieve King Malcolm. He shall witness the death of his son, and then my mother shall witness his death."

"Ossian?"

"NOW, IRWING!" the Prince commanded. "I shall wait no longer for my revenge!"

As Ossian acted on his plans for revenge, his mother brooded on her own thoughts high in the turrets of the black fortress. An occasional tear slid down her cheek as she moped about the dark room. She remembered when the bedchamber had been full of light and happiness. She stepped to the window, opening it to reveal the full moon. At the familiar sound of an Owl's screech, she watched as Ossian soared across the moon's glowing diameter. The silhouette reminded her once again of her early days with Jethart, before destiny had taken her down this dark path. She turned from the window to stand in front of his portrait hanging on the wall. She lovingly ran her hand down the side of the frame. The familiar motion had worn a groove in the heavy frame from a lifetime of loving strokes. As she stood there, she heard Jethart's words from so long ago echo in her heart.

"I do not teach you magic so that you may use it to harm others..."

She could control her emotions no longer. She sobbed uncontrollably as she crumpled to a heap at the foot of the portrait. "Oh, Jethart," she cried. "What have I done?"

137

Meanwhile, in the courtyard below, Lillith and a group of fairies stole their way from one dark space to the next, trying to hide from the revealing light of the full moon. At last they made it to a heavy side door. Lillith used her magic to release the lock and the group moved quickly through a wall of the dark fortress. They felt safe moving into the next level, but only for a moment. Lillith turned and came face-to-face with Irwing and the patrol he had gathered at Ossian's command. Reacting quickly, the fairies waved their small wands throwing streaks of fairy dust through the air. As the dust quickly covered the goblins, they sank to the floor under a spell of deep sleep.

Lillith released her breath. She didn't even realize she had been holding it, it had all happened so fast. With a wave of her hand to the fairies, they began to move forward again, but their magic had not gone entirely unnoticed. From his vantage point in the sky, Ossian had seen the brilliant streaks of light that accompanied the magic of the fairies' wands. He dived at the entourage but they moved quickly, staying just ahead of him. He screeched at the fairies, and the fairies shrieked in answer and prevented him from getting to Lillith as she raced toward the dungeon. Unable to follow them into the fortress, Ossian sped to the top of the turrets to sound his alarm.

Inside his cell, Roderick heard the commotion in the distance, and he struggled against his chains to try to see what was happening. The noise finally became loud enough to stir the sleeping imps that were guarding him. The creatures were barely on their feet when Lillith and the fairies burst into the dungeon area, throwing streaks of fairy dust in front of them. The imps immediately fell to the floor and back asleep. Lillith leapt over them and waved her wand at the lock on Roderick's cell door. It gave way, allowing her to enter.

Roderick's face registered his shock at being rescued by Lillith. She was the last person he had expected to see coming through his cell door. He'd expected his father's army…

"Quickly, Prince Roderick," she summoned. "We must hurry." With another wave of her wand, she broke his chains.

With no time for questions, Roderick followed her from the cell, and they raced back up the stairs to escape. Undaunted by a goblin sounding their escape at the top of the stairs, Lillith quickly tossed some fairy dust and dispatched him to sleep, as well. The pair escaped through the same side door Lillith had come through minutes earlier.

"This way to the stables," shouted Lillith. "Hurry!"

Roderick faltered in his step as the commotion of the screeching above drew his attention. He was horrified to see the great white owl and a pair of fairies in fierce battle. "We must help them!" he exclaimed.

"No! They protect us! We must leave quickly before the Dark Queen is roused. Hurry!"

With one last look at the horrific fight in the sky, Roderick fell in behind Lillith's lead.

High in the sky, the battle between feathers and fairy grew fiercer, as more fairies joined in against the razor-sharp talons of Ossian. He snapped and slashed, and tore at their wings, occasionally succeeding in dropping one from the sky. But for each one that fell, it seemed two more glowing sprites would join the fight. Knowing he needed reinforcements, Ossian pulled away from the fairies, circling the turrets and struggling to climb to the top. At last he reached his mother's balcony, but the Queen's window was closed. He flew against the window, beating at it with his wings to draw her attention. Moments later, she came to the glass.

"Ossian!"

He could see her shouting his name behind the panel of the window. Ossian began his transformation back to man as Elspeth unlocked the doors to her balcony. The Dark Queen watched in horror as her son was engulfed by the magic of the fairies without warning. He was instantly trapped in stone - a statue that was half-man, half-bird.

"NO!" she screamed as the protective rage of motherhood overtook her. She suddenly disappeared.

The scream from Elspeth seemed to shake the very ground that Lillith ran upon. "Hurry, Roderick," she urged. "She has seen us!"

"I need weapons," he shouted. He knew they could not outrun the magic that was engulfing the fortress. As quickly as he had asked, Magenta and Daphne granted his request. With a brilliant burst of light, Roderick was armed with a sword and shield.

Roderick glanced back up at Elspeth's balcony. She stood at its edge in all of her awful majesty, her staff held high. She formed runes that hung in the air as she wove a spell. Roderick watched, horrified, but too fascinated to look away.

"What shall we do?" cried Daphne.

Roderick looked to his right and saw that the fairies were trying to fend off a purple mist that rose from the ground of the courtyard. It threatened to swallow the group.

"Elspeth's magic is too strong," answered Lillith. "We must escape the confines of this fortress NOW! Come, Roderick," she ordered. "We shall lead you to safety."

Lillith grabbed his horse's bridle, and attempted to lead the animal through the ever-thickening mist. Daphne and Magenta hovered just ahead of her, trying to light the way, but it was futile. Within minutes, darkness had swallowed each of them, splitting them up.

High on the balcony, Elspeth continued her dark magic. Holding her staff close to her body, she let her head fall back and her form began to change.

Moments later on the ground, Lillith and Roderick stopped in their tracks as the mist parted to reveal a figure on horseback, wearing full armor and carrying a lance. He sat astride a jet-black horse that stamped at the ground, eager for battle. Lillith's eyes filled with horror as the figure raised his visor and stared at Roderick. She recognized that face.

"Identify yourself, Sir!" Roderick shouted. The figure did not answer. Lillith responded instead. "It is he, Roderick… the one your father defeated in battle!"

"You mean the Dark King?" he asked incredulously.

"Yes," she whispered.

"That cannot be! The Dark King died at my father's hand."

At last the man spoke, and Lillith recoiled at the cold tone of Jethart's voice.

"You are surprised, Prince Roderick? I return to complete the circle of life for life."

Words finished, he lowered his visor and dug his heels into the sides of the restless horse. Steam shot from its nostrils as it ran headlong toward Roderick. The Dark King lowered his lance into place and lightning bolts shot from the end of it.

Roderick kicked his own horse into action, moving just in time to avoid catastrophe. The two men continued in this dance for several minutes. The Dark King attacking, Roderick avoiding until his luck ran out. Finally, one of Jethart's lightning bolts landed close enough to knock Roderick's horse out from under him, sending him flailing to the ground.

Roderick searched frantically for the sword and shield that had been torn from his grasp in the fall. The mist continued to deter Roderick, and he once again barely avoided disaster as Jethart and his lightning bolts came charging at him. Roderick watched as the Dark King quickly turned the horse and charged again. But this time, a small figure leapt from the mists, swinging a sword. Jethart noticed the figure, but not before the sword made connection. It was enough to knock him to the ground, allowing Roderick time to find his sword.

As Roderick was retrieving his sword, the Dark King rolled over to reach his lance on the ground nearby. As he touched it, it transformed into a sword, and his armor dissolved, giving him the freedom to lift himself from the ground. As he rose, the small figure hit him with another blow of the sword. Roderick looked up in time to see that it was Lillith attempting to battle the Dark King. He knew she was no match for the powerful warrior, so he quickly rushed straight at Jethart.

The Dark King was now caught off guard. In swinging his sword at Lillith, he had allowed Roderick the opening he needed. Jethart's sword did not connect and when he turned, Roderick's charge drove his sword deep into Jethart's midsection. The Dark King's screams ripped through the air as he fell to his knees, and then to his back clutching at the heavy sword.

The mist dissipated as the Dark King struggled for air. Roderick stood over him, watching his agony and thinking of the words he would use to describe this moment to his father, when suddenly the Dark King began to transform. Roderick was frozen as Elspeth's true self was revealed.

"Roderick," she gasped. "Come…" She motioned for him to come to her side, but still he stood frozen.

"Do not fear. I could have killed you long before this. I… I will not harm you," she coughed and continued to struggle for breath.

Instinctively, Roderick knelt at her side and lifted her into his arms.

"You… You defeat me, Sir… You have defeated… the evil Dark Queen. You… shall be a… hero among your people," she gasped.

"No," he answered. "Not a hero. For the one I defeat is neither evil nor an enemy."

"Dear Roderick… You… were right." A tear slid down her pale cheek as she continued. "You were right. I… I sought vengeance on… your father. I should never… have taken it… out on you. Please… Forgive me…"

A cry of pain escaped her lips.

"Of course I forgive you," he whispered in her ear. "And I pray that you can forgive my father."

"Tell Ossian I…"

The Dark Queen fell to silence, as Lillith joined Roderick at her side.

"Lillith? Can you help her?" he begged. "I never intended to harm her. I didn't know."

"Don't blame yourself, Prince Roderick," Lillith answered. "You couldn't have known."

Lillith laid her hand across Elspeth's forehead, and took her hands into her own. "She is very weak," she observed. "Her wound may well be mortal."

"Can you do anything, Lillith? Please, do not let her die. She protected me when her son would have killed me. I owe her my life no matter what cruel intent she may have had."

"I shall do all I can to save her, Roderick. I do not wish to see her die either. You see… She is my sister, and we were once very close."

Magenta fluttered to Lillith's side, pulling the reins of a horse behind her. "Lillith, take her to the cottage. We will help you care for her there."

Lillith nodded. She rose and pulled the sword from Elspeth's body. Roderick helped her to lift Elspeth to the waiting horse, then solemnly watched as the sisters disappeared into the dark forest at the edge of the fortress. His thoughts were interrupted by Magenta's tiny voice.

"You have saved us all from Elspeth's dark power."

"I'm not so certain," he answered thoughtfully, "When the vengeance left her eyes, I... I felt she was as much a victim as my own mother. Had my mother been as strong, perhaps she would still be here.

"The past cannot be changed, Prince Roderick" observed Daphne who had joined them. "What matters now is that her dark reign has ended, and we must hurry to free Princess Ealasaid before anything more happens."

"The Princess," Roderick lamented. "I cannot free her from the bonds of death. I have won this battle, but I am still the one who has been defeated."

"What do you mean?" asked Daphne.

"Ealasaid is already dead, murdered by Elspeth's magic and hatred for my father."

"No!" Magenta fluttered to his side. "You are wrong. She is not dead!"

"But, she said..."

"She was wrong, Roderick," Daphne declared. "It's true Elspeth wove a spell of death, but Lillith was able to alter the spell that day. Ealasaid is not dead. She sleeps, Roderick. A deep sleep, filled with dreams of bliss, where she rests until awakened by true love's kiss."

"A kiss?" the Prince questioned.

"Yes, Prince Roderick. A simple kiss from one who loves her will save Ealasaid," Daphne whispered into his ear.

"If you love her, you must free her," whispered Magenta into the other.

Chapter 40
True Love's Kiss

Daphne and Magenta hastened to Rookskrieg Castle with Prince Roderick in tow. They led him into a courtyard where he observed the sleeping animals and guards.

"This way," Magenta urged.

Roderick followed her through the doorway, and traversed the passages and chambers of the castle, noticing the sleeping occupants along the way. He stopped in the throne room, and observed King Byron and Queen Isabelle.

"Why do they all sleep?" he asked.

"When Ealasaid fell into her deep slumber, we could not bear for our beloved King and Queen to see their daughter in such a state. A sprinkling of our dust, and…"

"They all fell asleep," Roderick replied.

"That's right," said Magenta.

Daphne flew in front of Roderick. "Come Sir… Your princess lies ahead."

Roderick followed the fairies through the passageway, the kitchen, and up the winding staircase. When he reached the open doorway of Ealasaid's chamber, he stopped, frozen at the sight of her beauty. Slowly, he approached the dais. When he reached the top, he sat on the edge of the bed and stared into the Princess' sleeping face. As the fairies fluttered above, he leaned over and tenderly kissed her ruby lips. Her eyes fluttered open and she sat up.

"What? … Wha…? Oh! I must have fallen asleep." She looked Roderick in the eyes. "I had the strangest dream… Is it time for the banquet?"

The young prince laughed heartily. "I certainly hope so! I've worked up an appetite!" He and the fairies laughed as Ealasaid looked on, puzzled.

Later, in the Great Hall, members of the court and servants in the castle began to awaken from their sleep.

Back at Dubh Rathgart, as the spell on Ealasaid broke, Ossian dissolved from stone into his human form. He stood on the balcony, surveying the courtyard. He saw his mother's staff on the ground in the distance. Transforming into the owl, he flew away.

Back in Rookskrieg Castle, everyone was finally awakened from their deep slumber, and the festivities began. Roderick escorted Ealasaid into the Great Hall and presented her to King Byron and Queen Isabelle. They hugged her, and all were joyful as the members of the court watched the reunion.

Chapter 41
Beginnings and Endings

The solitary white owl circled slowly over the battered courtyard of Dubh Rathgart. Ossian transformed back into his human form as he touched the ground, and knelt beside his mother's staff that rested in a pool of blood. He studied the area around it. All that remained were a few torn remnants of her royal robes. He could find nothing more of Elspeth.

"No... No..." he wept, as he gathered the scraps to his broken heart. He could only raise his head when a small, dark hand touched his shoulder. Ever faithful Irwing was at his side. The goblin laid his head on his Prince's shoulder and joined in his mourning for their beloved Queen. As morning broke, they were joined by other creatures of the Dark Realm.

Meanwhile, in the brightness of morning in the realm of Rookskrieg, Prince Roderick and Princess Ealasaid began the new day with a wedding ceremony. Their guests cheered as the two sealed their vows with a kiss, then retreated back up the aisle of the Chapel to begin the day's joyous celebrations.

But there was no celebrating in the Dark Realm. The goblins worked together to inter what was left of Elspeth next to her beloved Jethart. Ossian watched as the glass-covered black coffin holding the tattered remains of her robes was lifted into place at his father's side, and graced with a blanket of her favorite purple roses. Wails of mourning and tearful shrieks filled the burial crypt as the creatures of the Dark Realm marched through, paying their final respects to the Queen. Only Ossian remained dry-eyed as he stared vacantly at the procession passing his parents' tomb.

Meanwhile, Roderick and Ealasaid were enjoying a procession of a different kind. They stood happily side-by-side, greeting each of their guests in turn. King Malcolm suddenly cut into the line, placing himself directly in front of Roderick. He smiled proudly at his son, smugly content that the union of the realms of Talonsbay and Rookskrieg was now complete, and Elspeth destroyed. He extended his hand to his son in congratulations, but it was not accepted. He shrank back slightly at the cold stare Roderick gave him. Roderick pushed past his father and pulled Ealasaid along behind him. He led her to the center of the great hall and danced with her, trying his best to tune out the remarks of the guests...

> *"He is a hero"*
> *"Destroyed the Dark Queen single-handedly"*
> *"Following in his father's footsteps"*
> *"Saved Princess Ealasaid from certain death"*
> *"He will be a great king"*

Roderick did not want to hear their words, or be thought of in the same manner as his father. He now knew there was more to the story of the Dark Queen than the rest of the realm would ever know. For now, he only wanted to make plans with Ealasaid for their future, and forget about the past.

Chapter 42
The Dark King Rises

Time had passed slowly inside the walls of the black fortress. It seemed to Irwing that all the creatures of the realm had fallen into a dark sleep. They moved about, took care of business, went through all of the motions, but there was no life in them. It had been that way for months. Irwing made his way past the depressed creatures into the great hall where he found Ossian perched on the large black marble throne. It was obvious the young man was deep in thought.

Irwing tentatively approached him. "My King?" He was pleasantly surprised when Ossian looked up and met him with a smile. The young man's face had been a constant stoic mask of apathy since his mother's death.

"Irwing! I'm glad to see you."

"You are no longer sad, my King?" Irwing was thrilled to see life stirring once again in the man.

Ossian gave the goblin a thoughtful look before answering. "I shall always be sad at the loss of my mother, but it is time to move on." He rose from the dark throne and strode purposefully toward the front of the great hall. He spoke again before he exited through the heavy doors.

"It is time to take back all that has been stolen from our realm, Irwing. Bring me my mother's staff."

New life also stirred in the walls of Rookskrieg. Roderick and Ealasaid had made their home in the castle, and Roderick would soon take his place as King of the realm. In the meantime, they anxiously awaited the birth of their own child. Ealasaid thought it would be soon, perhaps with the next full moon.

But the full moon would bring more than the new family had bargained for, for high in the turrets of Dubh Rathgart, Ossian stood in the light of that moon. He held Elspeth's magic staff before him, the orb glowing a bright purple as he wove his spell. When at last he thrust the staff high into the air, sparks flew, thunder roared, and dark clouds rolled across the sky. In a flash of bright lightning, Ossian disappeared…

The End